Hell is a Skyscraper

A Trio of Novelettes

Hell is a Skyscraper
A Trio of Novelettes

Darliss Batchelor

Word in Due Season
Publishing, LLC

Hell is a Skyscraper
A Trio of Novelettes

Word in Due Season Publishing, LLC
P.O. Box 210921
Auburn Hills, Michigan 48321-0921
www.DarlissBatchelor.com

Cover Design by AMB Branding and Design
ambbranding@gmail.com

ISBN 13: 978-0-9829686-6-6
ISBN 10: 0-9829686-6-6

Library of Congress Control Number: 2014955029

Printed in the United States of America

This is a work of fiction. Any references or similarities to actual events, real people, living or dead, or to real locales are intended to give the novel a sense of reality. Any similarity in other names, character, places, and incidents if entirely coincidental.

Acknowledgments

I can't believe it! I am actually writing acknowledgements for my second book! This has truly been a dream come true for me. I have always been a reader. Now, it's my pleasure to write stories that others learn from and enjoy. I can only pray that what I write is half as enjoyable as what I've read by others. Books by favorites like Victoria Christopher Murray, Terry McMillan and Kimberla Lawson Roby serve as examples of great stories but also as a classroom for an emerging author such as myself.

I thank God for entrusting me with the gift of writing. I pray that each project serves the purpose for which He sent it.

I must also acknowledge my husband, Gregory Batchelor, for being a tremendous source of support. I appreciate him for his patience, consideration and love. Love you, Batch!

I must also express my thanks to Carol Lott and James Esnault for participating as readers for this project. Special thanks go to editor Alicia Street not only for improving the writing, but the writer as well.

I must say a big "God bless you" to every person who has supported me by asking, "When is the next book coming out?" There are times when I struggle as a writer. Then, God will send one of you to remind me that this is not for me anyway, but for others. I want you to know I don't take any of you for granted and I receive it all as love. I love you back!

Mother, May I

Chapter 1

Egypt rose to the sound of her alarm clock ringing. She couldn't believe it was time to start another day. She sat on the side of her bed and said a prayer for God's strength and guidance. She slid her feet into her slippers and padded down the hall toward her mother's room to determine if she was home. Egypt heard her leave the night before but didn't remember hearing her return. It really didn't matter if she was there or not because the outcome was the same for Egypt. She was responsible for seeing that her siblings got to wherever they needed to be. She did want to insure her mother was safe before she went to school. Slowly opening her mother's bedroom door, she realized it was empty, causing Egypt a bit of anxiety. Egypt turned and went to her room to wake up her little brother and sister.

Her sister, Shae, was seven years old and the most difficult to wake up, so Egypt started with her.

"Shae, wake up. It's time for school."

Shae responded by grumbling something about still being sleepy. She turned over, putting her thumb in her mouth, and went back to sleep. Egypt's tactic was to use Shae being ticklish to awaken her. Shae laughed and began to fight off her big sister.

"Get up, little girl. Do what you need to do in the bathroom. I'll come in the kitchen to fix your breakfast. You can pick what you want to eat."

"Okay!" Shae being able to pick her breakfast always got her moving a little quicker.

Egypt then jiggled Corey to awaken him. As usual, the three-year-old popped up out of his sleep like a jack-in-the-box. She laid him back down to check his pull-up for moisture. Egypt realized she would have to bathe Corey before they left the apartment though he'd had a bath the night before. She ran the water for his birdbath while she fixed Shae's chosen breakfast. Within an hour, everyone was ready to go.

She took Corey to Miss Smith next door and begged her to watch him until her mother returned or until she got out of school. Miss Smith obviously wanted to say no, but couldn't bear to inconvenience Egypt any more than the seventeen-year-old high school senior already was. She agreed to help Egypt once again and offered to feed the family after school if their mother wasn't home yet. Egypt boarded the bus that would take her and Shae to school. She and Shae read to each other until they reached the stop closest to Shae's school. She walked her little sister inside, then walked the few remaining blocks to her school.

Though Egypt had no children, she felt like she had three: Shae, Corey, and her mother. Egypt didn't complain though because she knew they all needed her. Her mother, Carolyn, was only fifteen when she had Egypt and she hadn't had a chance to be the carefree teenager she should have been at that age. Grandma Peete didn't allow her daughter to shirk her responsibility where Egypt was concerned. Parties, dates, ballgames, proms and the like were out. Grandma Peete said Mommy had given up her rights to all of that when she had the two minutes of fun with their Poppy, Desmond. So, Mommy seems to be having her fun now.

Egypt sat in her normal seat in her homeroom class. After announcements and attendance, the bell rang and the class left to begin their first subject of the day. By the end of the day, Egypt was exhausted. Not only had she stayed up late the previous night doing homework and studying for tests, Corey had been fussy and didn't want to settle down. Getting up this morning, shuffling everyone out of the door and making it through the school day were particularly tiring. Egypt had fallen asleep a few times during school. Her prayers were answered when the school allowed an early dismissal for Shae without too much fuss. She prayed her mother was home so she could catch a nap before she began her studies for the evening.

When Egypt reached her block, she noticed Miss Smith standing on her stoop apparently waiting for her. When Miss Smith noticed Egypt coming down the street, she went inside and returned with Corey.

"Hi, Miss Smith. Hey, Corey. Mommy didn't make it home yet?"

"Yes, she's in there. I saw her stumble down the street hours ago. She didn't look like she would be able to care for this little boy so I just kept him with me. I can't talk long because I have an appointment to get to."

"Thank you for watching Corey for me. I don't know what I would do if you weren't willing to watch him."

"I'm doing it because of you. Let me tell you a little something, young lady. Shae and Corey are not your responsibility. Your mother needs to step up and do what mothers do. The next time I see Carolyn I'm going to remind her that she needs to grow up and take care of her children. I know you have dreams Egypt. I know you have something you want to do with your life besides caring for your family and you should. You're going to have to get free of this load so you can live your own life."

Egypt walked the two doors to their home with Shae and Corey. She looked down at the two and realized how much she loved and cared for them. She couldn't imagine loving her own children any more than these two. Leaving them in the sole care of her mother just didn't seem like the right thing to do.

When they arrived at home, they all went to their mother's bedroom excited to see her. The children ran into the room and jumped on her bed. Groggily, their mother turned over and glared at her offspring. It was obvious she didn't want to be disturbed. Corey, unaware of his mother's mood, sat on her, craving her attention. Suddenly, she pushed him off her, letting out a grunt that further confirmed her displeasure revealing a wet spot. Apparently, Corey's overflowing pull-up needed changing.

"Get up off me, Corey!" Carolyn yelled as she pushed her little boy away from her. The little boy moved away from his mother. His downturned lips saddened Egypt.

"Corey needs his pull-up changed. That's all."

"Well, why are you telling me about it? Get him cleaned up while I take a shower. Change my sheets while you're at it. He probably got those wet too," Mommy said as she left her bedroom without even acknowledging Shae who was walking alongside her mother.

"Mommy, you want to see what I made in school today?"

"No, I don't have time right now. Show it to Egypt."

"I have studying to do tonight. I can't watch Corey and Shae."

"Well, you better find time to watch them because I think I have an appointment tonight. I don't know why you're studying so hard anyway. You're not going to need that education. You're going to do what people in our family have always done."

"I don't want to go on welfare."

"If your daddy would do better by y'all, we wouldn't have to be on welfare."

Egypt lay in bed that night seemingly unable to sleep. Egypt's thoughts overshadowed the soft snores of her siblings. Her mother's words kept running rampant through her mind. As miserable as they were, why would her mother act like it's okay to live like this? This was no way to live. Egypt had a desire for a better life. She'd never shared it with her mother because she didn't think she would understand. She would just make her dream seem silly.

Egypt dreamt of becoming a world-renowned journalist. She imagined herself traveling the world to exotic locales looking for and reporting the truth around the globe. She would be a cast member of a nationally televised news program. That's what she dreamt of doing when she had a few moments to herself.

The reality was she lived in a run-down two-bedroom house with her mother and two siblings. Truthfully, she was the one who was raising her little brother and sister. Her mother was missing in action most of the time. Egypt struggled to find time, space, and the quiet she needed to study as a high school student. How would she ever do it for college courses? The goal seemed unreachable based on her current circumstances and she didn't see where any of it would change soon.

Her mother's words about their father also spent some time galloping through her psyche. Egypt decided the next time she saw him, she would ask him why he didn't support them as a man should. He always spoke to Egypt about what a good man looks like and that was one of the things he mentioned. He would always say, "A good man is a provider!"

His second family lived in a five-bedroom house when they only needed four. They traveled on nice vacations, went out to dinner most of the time, and always had the latest and greatest of everything. Her father did have the three of them over sometimes, but their visitations with him were anything but consistent. It seemed unfair for them to struggle and his new family to be living the high life. Yes, this was something Egypt definitely would confront.

Chapter 2

The next day Egypt started her morning ritual. Though her mother was home, she refused to get up to help get everyone prepared for the day. She told Egypt she needed to take Shae to school and Corey to Miss Smith as usual.

Egypt went to wake Shae up and noticed the young girl seemed to have a fever. She went to the bathroom, located a thermometer, and coaxed her sister to let her take a reading. Shae's temperature was 102 degrees and she appeared to have the chills.

"Mommy, Shae's sick. She needs to go to the doctor. She can't go to school like this. She's too sick."

"What's wrong with her?"

"I don't know, but she's got a high fever and she's shaking like she's cold."

"She's just faking so she can stay home. Get her ready so she can go to school."

"But, Mommy, she's really sick. She can't fake a fever. Come and see for yourself."

"I said she's going to school! Now don't backtalk me."

Egypt closed the door to her mother's bedroom and returned to the room she shared with her siblings. She sat on her bed and watched as Shae trembled. Not sure what to do, she slipped on some shoes and a robe and went to talk to Miss Smith. Egypt was sure she would know what to do. The brisk wind sent chills through her own body as she ran to Miss Smith's door. She knocked and rang the doorbell hoping to gain entry into the warm apartment. The porch light came on informing Egypt of her success.

"What are you doing running around out here in your robe? You'll catch your death of cold out here. Come on in, child."

"Miss Smith, Shae is sick. Her temperature is 102 degrees and she can't go to school."

"No, it sounds like she's too sick to go to school. Is your mother home?"

"Yeah, but she says Shae still has to go to school. Shae is shaking like a leaf and I know the school will just send her home anyway. I don't know what to do."

"I'm going to tell you what you're going to do. You're going home and get yourself ready for school. Don't disturb Shae or Corey. It's past time for me to talk to your mother anyway. Just leave the door unlocked and I'll be right over as soon as possible."

"I don't know about that, Miss Smith. Mommy might get really mad at me."

"What else can you do? Shae cannot go to school and that's that. I'll make sure your mother knows this was my doing. Okay?"

"Okay. I guess I'll see you when you come over."

Egypt returned home and began to dress and prepare breakfast for herself. Just when she was getting ready to leave, Miss Smith walked in. She went straight to the bedroom where Shae and Corey were sleeping. She laid the palm of her hand over Shae's forehead. She then checked Corey to insure he didn't have a fever as well since the trio slept in such close quarters.

"Egypt, go on to school. I'll take care of everything here. Don't worry. I've got everything under control," Miss Smith assured Egypt. "This here is not your concern and it's going to stop today or else!"

"Or else what?" Egypt nervously asked not liking the sound of the "or else" part.

"Let's just pray we don't get to that."

"Okay. Thank you for coming over."

"You go on to school now." Miss Smith walked into the other bedroom in the house. "Carolyn, get up out of that bed and come see about your children."

"What are you doing here? Where is Egypt? I told her to take Shae to school."

"With a hundred-and-two-degree temperature? Really, Carolyn? I know you know better than that. What is your problem? Egypt has been bringing Corey over almost every day and you've been doing whatever you were big and bad enough to do."

"I don't see as it's any of your business, Miss Smith. These are my kids."

"It's my business because I'm taking care of your kids while you're out having a good time. You're right about one thing though. They are your kids and you need to act like it."

"Where is Egypt again?"

"I sent her to school. She couldn't take Shae because she's sick and I'm tired of watching Corey when you're here and can do it. Now get up out of that bed. You need to change these sheets and spray this room down. It smells like something crawled up in here and died."

Egypt closed the door behind her as she left. She prayed all the way to school that her mother wouldn't be angry with her when she returned from school. Miss Smith promised she would take care of things, but Egypt just hoped she wouldn't end up paying the price.

***

This was a good day for Egypt. Just being a normal senior in high school was wonderful. She didn't have to worry about picking up Shae and Corey. She knew they'd be taken care of even if Miss Smith ended up having to do it.

Egypt's concern was her mother. Egypt didn't understand her mother's mentality. It wasn't clear to her why she didn't want any better for herself or her offspring. She seemed content going to the mailbox looking for her check, hanging out all night, then sleeping all day leaving Egypt to take care of everything else.

Egypt slowly entered the house not sure of what she would encounter. She heard music playing and what sounded like her mother's voice singing along. She walked past the kitchen and noticed her mother doing something she hadn't done in a very long time. She appeared to be cooking a meal. Egypt thought she might be dreaming. This could not be happening. She turned to go check on Corey and Shae. Shae was lying in bed reading a book and Corey was napping.

"How are you feeling, Shae?"

"I feel better. Mommy and Miss Smith took me to the doctor. They gave me some pink medicine and said it'll help me feel better."

"That's good, Shae. I was worried about you all day."

Egypt returned to the kitchen and greeted her mother.

"Hi, Mommy."

"Hi, Egypt."

"What are you doing?"

"You haven't seen me do this in so long that you forgot what it looks like?"

"I guess."

"I'm cooking for my family. That's what I'm doing."

"Mommy, I'm sorry for going to Miss Smith this morning. I just didn't know what to do."

"That's all right. Miss Smith helped me understand some things."

"You're not mad at me?"

"No, I can't be mad at you for being so spoiled."

"Spoiled? Did you say I'm spoiled?"

"Yes. See, when I was your age I was just like you. I took care of my brothers and sisters. But I understood how blessed I was to have a place to live and food to eat."

"Oh." This was news to Egypt.

"So, I was just thinking you need to do something to kick in around here. Don't you think?"

"I guess so," Egypt hesitantly responded, feeling as though she was walking into a trap of some sort.

"I'm glad you agree."

"Okay. I have some homework to do."

"No, not so fast. See, I didn't get to tell you that by the time I was your age, I had already dropped out of high school so I could raise you."

"Really?" Egypt didn't like where this appeared to be going.

"Really. I expect you to help too. I didn't get a choice, but I'm going to give you one. You can help me with Corey and Shae or you'll have to move out. I'm not going to struggle to take care of some selfish somebody."

• • •

"You're going to put me out if I don't keep taking care of Shae and Corey?"

"That's right. If you're so grown you don't think you have to do anything to help, then you must be grown enough to live on your own. You'll just have to quit school and get a job. If you want to do that, you can stay here. At least that way you'll be helping."

"Mommy, I can't quit school. I'm about to graduate."

"I know you think you're about to graduate and leave us to go to some college where they'll fill your head full of that same stuff they fed your daddy. You're just like him. Thinking you're better than everybody else."

"I never felt I was better than anybody."

"Yeah well, he's selfish too. He lives in that big house with his nice sweet little family while we're barely making it. That's what college taught him. He doesn't have to take care of his own."

Egypt realized this was a problem between her parents, but somehow she was stuck in the middle. Her dilemma was figuring out how to get out of it without becoming a high school dropout living on the street.

The next morning Egypt went about her normal morning routine. Corey stayed home with Mommy because she didn't want to hear Miss Smith's mouth on the subject. At least Egypt didn't have to worry about dealing with Corey. That was one thing off her plate.

"Come on, Shae. We're running a little late today. I need to get you in here quickly so I can get to school at least close to on time." Egypt and Shae jogged to the door to Shae's school where Shae's school principal met them.

"Good morning, Shae," Mrs. Riley said. "Egypt, can I talk to you for a minute?"

"Sure. Shae, go on to the cafeteria. I'll see you after school." After Shae skipped down the hall, Egypt returned her attention to Mrs. Riley. "Is everything okay with Shae? Oh, I have a doctor's note about her absence."

"I'll take the note and pass it on to her teacher to record."

"Okay, is that it?"

"No, there's something else I need to inform you of. You're dropping Shae off a little too early. The earliest students are allowed in the building is 8:15 unless they're in our latchkey program. It's not even 7:00 yet."

"I have to drop her off on my way to the high school. If I bring her at eight o'clock I'll be really late for school."

"I understand your predicament, but we have a schedule to follow here. If you'd like, I can give you the information about latchkey. If that's an option for you, we can get that set up quickly. Otherwise, this is the last day I can let Shae come this early. Follow me to the office and I'll give you that pamphlet."

"Um, Miss Riley, I'm really running late this morning."

"No problem. I'll put it in Shae's backpack right now."

"Thank you, Miss Riley. I'll make sure my mom sees it."

"Have a good day, Egypt. I'll see you later."

"Thanks. You have a good day too."

Egypt arrived at school and ran past her locker to her homeroom, sliding into her seat just as the bell rang. During attendance and other preliminaries, she thought about her new predicament. How would she get Shae to school and then get to school on time herself? She was sure the latchkey program would cost money she certainly didn't have, and based on her mother's comments, Mommy didn't have it either. Her mother had made Egypt's options clear. Neither option was very desirable. Mrs. Riley's announcement this morning seemingly pushed her toward one option more than the other. Since she couldn't put Shae in latchkey and her mother surely wouldn't let her off the hook for taking Shae to school, Egypt concluded she would have to quit school. That was the only way. The bell rang signaling the end of homeroom and the beginning of first hour class. As she walked past the teacher's desk, she tapped Egypt on the shoulder.

"Can I talk to you a minute?" Mrs. Matlin asked.

Now what? Egypt thought to herself.

"It's okay, Egypt. It's good news."

"All right." Egypt said as she followed Mrs. Matlin, who led her back to her desk.

Mrs. Matlin moved some things around on her desk until she came across a folder with Egypt's name on it. She smiled as she handed the folder to Egypt and waited patiently for Egypt to view its contents.

Egypt opened the file and saw her application materials for a journalism scholarship. In the back of the folder was a letter from the grantors of the scholarship. Her eyes focused on the words on the page. They granted Egypt the scholarship. All she had to do was accept it and the money she so desperately needed for school was hers.

"Congratulations! I'm so proud of you." Noticing Egypt's lack of enthusiasm, she directed her student to take a seat she pulled closer to the desk. "Talk to me. I thought you would be happy about this."

"Mrs. Matlin, I don't know if I'm going to be able to go to college."

"You're in and you've got the money. What's standing in your way?"

"I've got some personal family problems to work out. I don't even know if I'll finish high school."

"What's going on? Maybe I can help. I'd hate to see you pass up this opportunity."

"I might have to quit school to help my family. I don't want to, but I don't think I have any other choice."

"I see." Mrs. Matlin rose from her seat and went to close the classroom door. She returned to Egypt and asked a question. "Egypt, what do you know about prayer?"

"I pray all day every day. My Grandma Peete, taught me about it."

"Let's pray right now and ask God to work this out for you. Okay?"

"That's a good idea. Let's do that."

The two bowed their heads as Mrs. Matlin prayed a brief prayer for God to provide a solution for Egypt's concerns.

"I'll write you a pass to your first hour class. Don't worry, Egypt. I believe God is going to make it so you can graduate and take this scholarship."

Egypt felt the weight of her decision lift from her shoulders. She knew God could handle the situation. That's what Grandma Peete always told her. Egypt's mind went back to a conversation she had with Grandma Peete years ago before she passed away. Her words were indeed prophetic. Egypt could almost hear them now.

"You got to hold on to your dreams. There are people who will try to snatch your dreams because they lost hope in their own. I call them dream snatchers. They want to keep you from reaching your goal. God showed me you're gonna make it but you gonna have to fight for it. Don't let them steal your dream, gal."

A smile came to her face as she realized her dream was still viable. God would come through for her.

. . .

Chapter 3

Egypt picked Shae up from school and immediately looked for the latchkey program information. She found it and flipped through it to find what she was most interested in…the price. Just as she thought, this wasn't a free program and her heart sunk. No way was that going to happen. On the bus home, Egypt began to think about what her life would be like without a high school diploma. It wasn't the life she dreamed of each night as she fell asleep. Why did her life have to turn out this way?

Egypt's mother appeared to be living her childhood now. Her father was absent and didn't seem to care. Egypt realized she might have stumbled on the solution to her problem. Her father might be able to help with childcare for Shae so Egypt wouldn't have to leave school. After all, he hadn't been involved in their lives physically and apparently, he hadn't been participating financially either. It was certainly worth a try to speak to him. She would stop at Miss Smith's house and ask if she could use her phone to call him since their house phone wasn't working. Maybe he would pick her up so she could talk to him about his lack of support and helping her with Shae.

***

Egypt stood out on the sidewalk in front of her house and waited for her father to show up. She wanted to avoid the fights that typically occurred when her parents came face-to-face with each other. Egypt often wondered how they stood each other long enough to produce three children. Just then, she spotted her father pulling up in his big black luxury SUV. He stopped in front of her and unlocked the door for her to get in. After their initial greeting, the two mostly rode in silence aside from a little light bantering.

"I sense you wanted to talk to me about something in particular. Am I right?"

"Yes, you're right."

"Well, do you want to talk now?"

"I'd prefer to sit down and talk so we can really communicate."

"Okay. You want to go to the house or do you want to go somewhere else?"

"Will we be able to talk in private at your house?"

"Sure, we can make that happen."

Egypt always felt jealousy when she saw the stately home where her father and his second family lived. It was in a beautiful gated community with a pool, tennis courts and clubhouse for the inhabitants. She watched as her father pushed the button over the rearview mirror, which caused the garage door to lift, revealing a bright shiny new vehicle.

"Is that a new car?" Egypt asked.

"Yes. Why?" her father responded.

"Just asking. It's nice."

Egypt and her dad walked from the garage into a space called a mudroom where she had to remove and leave her shoes. On the other side of the mudroom was the kitchen where her stepmother was tossing a salad.

"Well, hello, Egypt! I didn't know you were coming today," Egypt's stepmother, Tara, said.

"Honey, Egypt and I are going to head to the office to talk for a bit."

"But I was just about to put dinner on the table."

"You and the kids go ahead and eat. I'll eat later. Egypt would you like something to eat?"

Egypt eyed the food and wanted to dive in headfirst because she was so hungry. She and her siblings didn't get too many meals outside of school so the availability of food tempted her greatly. However, she knew her mother would have a fit if she ate at her father's house. So in order to avoid confusion, Egypt declined.

Egypt and her father walked through the great room and up the stairs to the second level. They proceeded past five bedrooms and into a room at the end of the hall Egypt never knew existed. Her father closed the door behind them as Egypt sunk into the deep burgundy leather sofa. Her father sat down in a desk chair that he pulled up close to her and waited for her to begin.

"I don't know where to begin, there's so much to say, Egypt said.

"What is it? It seems really serious." Desmond asked.

"It is serious. I need to know if we can keep this between us."

"I'm not going to promise that because I don't know what's going on," Desmond said as he shook his head.

"Mommy wants me to drop out of school."

"What? Why would she want you to do that?" Poppy yelled.

"She said I need to pitch in to help take care of the family."

"What do you mean?"

"I'm responsible for getting Shae ready for school, dropping her off and picking her up. Most of the time, I have to tend to her and Corey after school too. I try to pull some scraps of food together to feed them. I bathe them and put them to bed. Sometimes in the morning, I have to drop Corey off at Miss Smith's house before I leave," Egypt explained.

"Where is your mother when you're doing all of this?"

"Sometimes she's home in her room and sometimes she's out somewhere. Miss Smith came by and had a talk with her about everything and Mommy told me I still had to do all of this stuff or I had to leave. She said even if I have to drop out of school to do it, I had to contribute somehow."

"I didn't know all this was going on." Desmond dropped his head.

"That's something else I wanted to ask you about. Why aren't you more involved? It seems like you don't care. Mommy said you don't love us like you do your other kids."

Desmond rolled his eyes. "I see Carolyn is spreading her venom. That couldn't be farther from the truth. I care about the three of you and I used to care deeply for your mother. The problem is Carolyn is bitter. She's angry that we didn't work out and that I moved on."

"I understand that, but why did you cut yourself off from me, Shae, and Corey? We didn't have anything to do with that."

"You're right. I shouldn't have allowed that to happen. It just got to the point I was tired of fighting with Carolyn just to talk to or see you. Honestly, I took the easy way out and apparently, you felt abandoned. I never meant for that to happen."

"Look at how you and your other family are living. You know how we live. Your new kids have the best of everything. Whatever they need they have it and they get most of what they want. Do you know our phone isn't working right now? We don't have heat many days. We are really struggling. Mommy said we wouldn't have to do without so much if you would pay some kind of child support."

"Is that what she said? Stay right there. I want to show you something." Poppy got up and went to a closet in the office. He grabbed a metal box off a shelf at the top of the closet and set it on a table. He motioned for Egypt to sit in a chair already stationed at the table and began to pull stacks of paper out of the box. He took the rubber band off one of the stacks and placed the small rectangular pieces of paper in front of Egypt. The first thing Egypt noticed was the word "receipt" printed on top of each of the papers. Flipping through them, she recognized her mother's signature on each of the ones she viewed.

"I don't understand. What are these?"

"I have been paying your mother every two weeks to help you all even when she wouldn't let me see you."

"But Mommy said…"

"I know what she told you. I knew these would come in handy one day. I had your mother sign a receipt before I would give her any money. Every time."

Egypt looked at several more receipts and verified her mother's signature was indeed on each one. She also noted the amounts and realized something was very wrong.

"I was concerned she might try to take me to court for child support one day and I wanted to have proof of what I've been doing over the years."

"But why would Mommy lie?" Egypt asked as she fell back in her seat.

"I don't know. You'll have to ask her."

"What is she doing with all of this money?"

"Again, you need to ask her."

"I don't know what this all means but I need your help. I can't drop out of school. I just got a scholarship and if I don't graduate, I can't go to college."

Poppy smiled. "I'm glad to hear you say you don't want to quit. What do you want to major in?"

"I want to major in journalism. That's my dream." Egypt beamed.

Desmond took Egypt's hands. "We're going to have to figure out a way to take some of this load off of your shoulders so you can get your diploma. If your mother won't change her mind, I guess that means you've got to leave her house."

"If I leave home, where will I go?"

"You'll come live here with us. What do you think about that?"

"I don't want to leave Shae and Corey behind. Who'll take care of them?"

"That's for your mother and me to figure out. You've already had to handle more responsibility than you should."

Biting her lip, Egypt glanced toward the office door. "Don't you have to talk to your wife about that?"

"Let me handle that end of it."

"Well, let me think about that. Leaving Shae and Corey is difficult to consider. I don't know if I trust Mommy to take care of them the way they need to be cared for."

"I'm going to have to talk to your mother about all this. If necessary, I may have to get the courts involved to insure all three of you are taken care of."

"You can't talk to Mommy! She'll be so upset with me for talking to you about what's going on!" Egypt cried. "I shouldn't have said anything. Just forget it. I'll figure it out another way."

"No, you won't, Egypt. The adults are going to handle it and let you get on with your life. You should be thinking about the prom, senior pictures, and moving into your college dorm, not worried about Corey and Shae. I'm going to speak to Carolyn and see if we can handle this between the two of us. In the meantime, forget about leaving high school right now and give me some time. This is all going to work out. Don't worry about it."

***

"Shae, I'm going to tell you a secret. Do you think you can keep this secret?"

"I can keep a secret," Shae said bouncing on the bed with excitement.

• • •

"You can't tell anyone, even Mommy or Miss Smith."

"I won't."

Egypt sat on the bed beside Shae and pulled her close. "I might be moving in with Poppy."

"Why?" Shae asked looking up at her big sister.

"I might have to move out of here."

"What about me and Corey?" She began to cry.

"You'll be okay," Egypt said hugging Shae.

"No, we won't. Mommy doesn't take care of us like you do."

"Don't worry. Poppy said he was going to take care of everything."

"Oooh, you talked about house business outside of the house. You know Mommy doesn't like that. She's going to be mad," Shae said.

"She won't be mad, Shae, because you said you would keep this secret, and I'm not going to tell her. How is she going to find out if we don't tell her?"

"I can't believe you would run off and leave us. I thought you loved us." Shae placed her thumb in her mouth.

"I do love you. You're making me feel bad."

"If you really cared, you would take us with you. You wouldn't go away but you are."

"I shouldn't have told you about this. I wasn't trying to upset you. I love you, Shae, and I know you know that. I didn't want you to be surprised if I moved out. Don't be mad at me."

Shae sat quietly for a few minutes as she thought about the information her big sister had given her. Finally, she looked up at Egypt and smiled.

"I could never be mad at you. I'll miss you if you go. You promise you won't forget me and Corey?"

"I could never forget you. You'll see me so much it'll be almost like I never left," Egypt assured Shae with a hug.

"So you went over to your daddy's house and spilled your guts, huh?" Egypt and Shae looked up at their mother as she slid, unnoticed, into the room.

"What are you talking about, Mommy?" Egypt asked, though she knew the answer already.

"I overheard you and Shae talking. Shae go in the kitchen and see what Corey's doing."

"Mommy, I didn't know what else to do. You gave me an ultimatum and I panicked. What did you expect me to do?"

"All you had to do was make a decision. But no, you had to go run and tell Poppy," Carolyn said as she entered the room.

"I had to talk to somebody," Egypt explained.

"No, you didn't. You know the rule. What happens in this house stays in this house. I let you slide with talking to Miss Smith, but I can't overlook you going to talk to your father." Carolyn said as she shook her head.

"I did what I felt was best. Mommy, I can't drop out of school. I got a scholarship for college, but I have to graduate in order to take advantage of it. The school won't let me drop Shae off early anymore, so I'll have to miss at least my first hour class in order to drop her off at the appropriate time. I just can't do it anymore." Egypt felt a tear drop.

"Well, I understand that. Here's the problem. You absolutely can't live in my house and not help me some kind of way. I'm not going to let you make me look bad. I'm not asking too much. However, you just can't do it anymore. Let me tell you something. When you leave this house, you cannot come back. I won't even allow you to visit. I won't allow your sister and brother to speak to or see you. If you or your Poppy presses that issue, I'll go to court and tell them whatever I have to in order to keep you both from being in their lives. Your daddy doesn't do anything to help me take care of you and you crawling up behind him. That's a shame after all I've done for you," Carolyn said pointing a stiff finger at her eldest daughter.

"Since you mentioned it, what do you do with that money Poppy's been giving you for us?"

"What money?" Carolyn rubbed her hands down her legs.

"I saw the receipts, Mommy. I know he's been paying you all this time while you've been saying he's a deadbeat," Egypt said with folded arms.

"What receipts?" Carolyn began to fidget.

"The receipts Poppy had you sign every time he gave you money."

"I don't know what kind of stuff your father is trying to pull, but he never gave me anything except a donation on the three of you."

"I don't believe you. I saw them and it's clearly your signature that's on them."

"You need to think about what you're saying, little girl, and who you're saying it to. I won't stand here and have you call me a liar. Poppy's the liar. He's living high on the hog over there with his little family and we're over here barely making it. Why would I choose to live like this if I didn't have to? Think about that." Carolyn rushed away.

Egypt hadn't looked at it from that perspective. Why would she live here if she could do better? Egypt would speak to her father again and ask some more questions.

• • •

Chapter 4

Poppy pulled up in front of the house and honked the horn. Carolyn stood in the door glaring at him with her arms crossed as Shae happily ran out of the house and jumped in the truck. Egypt slowly followed, sensing the ill will flowing between her parents. She regretted causing this all to come to a head, but at the same time, she felt a bit of relief. The truth was out and everyone knew what was going on. More than that, Poppy followed through on his promise to take care of things. He came every morning to pick Shae and Egypt up for school, relieving Egypt of the responsibility to handle the early morning schedule. He paid for Shae to go to latchkey, which allowed Egypt to arrive at school on time each morning. At the end of the day, Egypt caught the bus to her father's house and Tara, their stepmother, picked Shae up and took her home with her. When Poppy got off work, he took them both home to keep confusion from breaking out between Tara and Carolyn. Corey stayed with his mother instead of Miss Smith and everything seemed to be going well.

"Egypt, I want you to tell your Poppy to come in for a minute. You come with him. I got something I need to say."

"Okay."

Egypt walked out to the truck and relayed her mother's message. Father and daughter's eyes exchanged a silent message: one questioning the other what was going on. Poppy nodded and silently exited the vehicle. Shae sat in the truck and played with the radio while the impromptu meeting took place.

"Good morning, Carolyn. How are you?"

"I've been better." She sneered, as she looked at Desmond from head to toe.

"I'm running a little late this morning. What do you need?" Desmond asked.

"You're going to sit down and listen to what I have to say. That's the least you could do since you abandoned us."

"Carolyn, you know what happened. You know I didn't abandon you. Don't start."

"I know no such thing."

"Look, can we make this quick? I've got to get the girls to school so I can get to work."

Carolyn placed one hand on her hip, pointed with the other and said, "I don't appreciate what you're trying to do. This girl thinks her stuff don't stink because you and your little wife are planting all that stuff in her head. Don't think I don't know she's picking my kids up, feeding them all kinds of fancy food and smoothies and stuff. My kids don't eat like that."

"The girl has aspirations. You do remember what that's like, don't you? You had aspirations, too."

"Aspirations don't mean a thing and they sure don't make one person better than the other."

"What's the point? We've got to get going."

"Since you want to be all father-like all of a sudden, you're going to have to do it twenty-four seven. Egypt, you need to get your stuff and get out of my house. Tonight. I no longer want you here. I don't have a need for an ungrateful mouth to feed," Carolyn said pointing motioning toward the door.

"Mommy, please don't."

"It's too late. You brought all of this drama to my door and I can't deal with that. You have hurt me for the last time."

"I'm sorry. Don't make me leave. I'll figure it out. Just don't put me out," Egypt cried as her dad held her close.

"Carolyn, I didn't think you could get any lower. How can you just tell your daughter to get out of the house? Do you know what this will do to her?" Desmond yelled.

"She should've thought about that before she complained about her unbearable living conditions."

"You caused this drama all because you didn't want to be a responsible mother. This is not her fault."

"Well, I really don't care who you, of all people, think is at fault. She has to go. Now, Poppy, what are you going to do about this? She can't come live with you and your little picture-perfect family?" Carolyn questioned as a huge smile revealed itself.

"We've already discussed it. All of my children are welcome to live with us. Do you want to send Corey and Shae, too? We have enough room for all of them."

Egypt exhaled as she watched Carolyn's grin turn into a grimace. She was ecstatic her father proved he wasn't the lousy self-centered man her mother made him out to be.

"No, I'm not letting you take my babies. You can have the ungrateful one, but the others are my insurance policy."

"Insurance policy? What do you mean by that?"

"As long as I have them, you'll have to deal with me, and I promise I'm going to make your life a living hell." Carolyn sneered.

"You don't even want these kids. You just want to give me a hard time. That's pitiful." He sighed. "You know, I'm tired of trying to reason with you. Bring it on, Carolyn. Do whatever you've got to do."

"I will. Now you just make sure you get what little Egypt has in my house out tonight."

As the argument escalated, Egypt shrank into a corner of the living room bawling, wondering how things had gone so badly so quickly.

Shae entered the room looking between her parents as they yelled at the top of their lungs at each other. She noticed Egypt sobbing and began to cry herself. As if on cue, Corey awoke and began to cry in the other room. Chaos had broken out and everyone was involved.

"Stop it, please! I can't take it!" Egypt yelled trying to get the situation under control.

"This is your fault, Egypt. Now, you got Mommy and Poppy all upset," Shae screamed.

· · ·

"Calm down. Girls, get in the truck. Carolyn, we'll have this discussion later when it's just the two of us," Desmond directed. After Egypt and Shae exited, he went to check on Corey and insured he was on his way back to sleep.

"Bye, Carolyn," he said calmly as he left to get his daughters to their destinations before going to work.

"I'm sorry you two had to hear all of that, but your mother and I will get through this. I don't want either one of you to worry about what's going on. As I said before, the adults are going to handle adult business. You guys just be kids."

"Egypt is the one who should be saying she's sorry. She makes Mommy upset all the time."

"Why do I need to apologize?" Egypt asked turning toward the backseat.

"All Mommy asked you to do is take care of me and Corey, but you can't even do that. You're too busy trying to be all high and mighty. Mommy told me that's what happens when you go off to college like you're trying to do" Shae said.

"I'm just trying to do what everybody my age is doing. I can't take care of you and become the journalist I want to be, too. I can't handle it all," Egypt responded.

"I'm not talking to you anymore, Egypt. I'm mad at you."

"I've heard enough. Shae, this is not your sister's fault. She's not your mother. Your mother should be taking care of all three of you. That's her job and not Egypt's. There's no need for you to be upset with her about any of this. Do you understand?" Desmond declared.

"Yes, sir. But what are we gonna do about Mommy? She was crying when we left."

"I don't know. Mommy and I will figure it out though, okay?"

"Okay."

Later that evening Egypt stood in her new room at her father's house. The room was a beautiful shade of lavender. Though she hadn't chosen the color, it suited her just fine. There was a white four-poster bed with a beautiful down comforter over it complete with coordinating bed skirt and pillows. Various throw rugs with prints in shades of purple, pink, and blue adorned the beautiful wood floors.

"This is a far cry from where I laid my head last night," she mumbled as she sat her belongings on the bed in order to unpack.

"Hi," Tara said as she slowly entered the room. "Do you need anything?"

"No, I think I'm okay. Just trying to get settled in."

"Is that all you brought?" Tara said referring to the few bags sitting on the bed.

"Well, I didn't have much anyway and this is all Mommy would let me take. She made me leave some stuff."

"Oh. Well, there are plenty of hangers in the closet. You can also use any of the dresser drawers you need. This space is all yours to use. I'll help you get organized."

"Okay."

Tara and Egypt worked together to put Egypt's things away. Then Tara showed her the attached bathroom that was all hers as well. Egypt didn't even know there was a bathroom in this bedroom. It seemed there were several rooms in this house she didn't know existed.

"You know, Egypt. Desmond told me about what you've been going through. I think you're a wonderful young woman. You are not what your mother said you were. Don't accept that as the truth of who you are."

"I don't know what makes her get so mad at me."

"I think you remind your mother of all that she could have done but didn't. That's no excuse, but I think she might even be a little jealous," Tara stated as she placed Egypt's tops in a drawer.

"Jealous? I'm her daughter."

"Sometimes parents regret the decisions they made in life. Many parents want to see their kids do better than them. Some parents don't. You just happen to have a parent that isn't very excited about you going off to college and pursuing a career. You haven't done anything wrong."

Egypt sat on the edge of the bed. "I'm going to have to spend some time trying to understand that. It doesn't make any sense to me."

Tara took a chair close by. "If I can help you, let me know. In the meantime, you and I are going shopping this weekend to make sure you have everything you need. Does that sound good?"

"I guess. I'm still a little worried about Shae and Corey though. I feel like I abandoned them. I just want them to be okay." Egypt dropped her head into her hands.

"I know, honey. Desmond is working on making sure they'll be okay. He loves you kids, too, contrary to what your mother said, and so do I. Let me know if you need anything." Tara rose from the chair she'd been sitting in to leave the room.

"Thank you. Um..."

"Yes, Egypt?" Tara turned to faced Egypt.

"I don't know what to call you."

"You can call me Tara. That's fine with me."

"But the other kids call you Mom."

"I'm going to leave that to you. You call me whatever you feel comfortable calling me."

"So if I called you 'hey you' that would be okay?" Egypt joked, finally relaxing a bit.

"That would be fine, but I know you wouldn't do that," Tara laughed as she left the room and closed the door.

As Egypt lay in bed that night, she pondered her situation. She would never have believed she would end up in this predicament. All she could think about was Shae and Corey. How the argument earlier in the day had affected them so deeply. She heard Corey's cries and Shae's yelling repeatedly in her head. The terrible things her mother said about her also seemed to be on instant replay as well. It was only a small consolation that her mother's comments weren't true. Or were they? Was she ungrateful? Was Shae right? Should Egypt just be the caregiver her mother expected her to be?

Egypt could've just dropped out of high school and gotten a job. That solution would work for everyone involved—except Egypt. That would mean a huge sacrifice. No college and no dream career as a journalist. That was just too much to bear. Perhaps, she could get a GED later and go to school then. However, money for school would probably be an issue.

Would there ever be a chance for her to live her life the way she always dreamed? Would her mother ever be willing to step up and be the parent she needed to be? Only God knew the answer to that question. All of that was probably water under the bridge.

Her mother had thrown her out anyway, so what was Egypt left to do? She decided to focus on the positive that could come out of what happened. She no longer had the responsibility for her younger siblings and her mother. She was no longer required to do all of the cooking and cleaning. She was confident the lights, phone and heat would always be on in Poppy and Tara's house. Egypt loved the idea of having her own space and time to do her homework and study without interruption. Poppy already told her that was her only job.

Now, she could take the scholarship and get on with moving in the direction her heart was leading. Whether she could do that without feeling guilty about leaving her mother and siblings behind was the question. She heard Grandma Peete's words about the battle and realized this must be it. The fight was between her destiny and her family.

Chapter 5

Poppy and Egypt pulled up to pick Shae up as they'd been doing for weeks. Egypt walked to the door and rang the bell since she could no longer access her former home any other way. Her mother answered the door and glared at Egypt.

"Good morning!" Egypt exclaimed more excitedly than she really felt.

"Hi. Wait here," her mother mumbled angrily.

"Can I come in? I just want to look in on Corey," Egypt explained as she stepped back out of the door.

"I told you that was over when you left."

"But you let me see him since then."

"Count yourself lucky. I'm standing by what I said. Besides, you don't care about us anyway." Carolyn leaned against the doorjamb with her arms crossed.

"How can you say that? That's not true."

"Yeah well, you're living over there with Desmond and Tara, aren't you?"

"That's because you told me I had to leave."

"I recall no such thing. As a matter of fact, I've been talking to some people about charging your Poppy with something called parental kidnapping."

"Why are you doing this Mommy?"

"Because I can and I want to."

"Bye, Mommy. I'll see you later," Shae said as she arrived at the door with an attitude bigger than her backpack.

"Bye, baby. I'll see you when you get home from school. I think we'll order pizza tonight. I know it's your favorite."

"Yeah. I love pizza."

"Anything for my favorite daughter. Go on ahead so you're not late for school," Carolyn said as she gazed at Egypt.

Shae walked out the door past Egypt as though she weren't even present.

"How are you doing?" Egypt said as the two walked to the truck.

"Fine."

"Is that all you have to say?"

"Yes."

"Okay," Egypt said dejectedly.

• • •

The ride to school was tense and silent. Shae was apparently committed to being upset with Egypt and wasn't much happier with Poppy. She ran into her school ahead of her father without so much as a goodbye to her big sister. This was becoming unbearable for Egypt.

When Egypt arrived at her homeroom class, Mrs. Matlin was waiting at the classroom door, apparently, for Egypt.

"Let me talk to you for a minute," Mrs. Matlin requested.

"Yes, ma'am," Egypt responded.

"How is everything going? You've been looking down lately."

"Things are going okay, I guess." Egypt dropped her head.

"Have things gotten better at home?"

"Yes and no. Actually, I'm living with my father now. I've been there for a few weeks."

"Is that a good thing or not?"

"It's a good thing for me, but I'm really concerned about my mother, my little brother, and sister."

"I see. So what are your plans?" Mrs. Matlin asked.

"I don't know if I'm staying where I am or if I'm going to try to go home. It's a difficult decision. My mom and sister are mad at me. I can't see my little brother. That hurts." A lone tear fell.

"I guess that would be tough. I know you love your family, but at some point you have to begin making decisions that are good for you, too." Mrs. Matlin placed her hand on Egypt's arm.

"I know but I feel so guilty."

"I understand. I hate to add more pressure, but we really need to know soon what you're going to do about the scholarship. If you're not going to take it, we need to notify them. That way someone else can take advantage of it."

"Okay. I'm going to keep praying about this and I'll let you know what I decide as soon as I know."

"That's fine. Egypt, I hope you don't let this opportunity pass you by. This doesn't happen very often anymore. I can't think of anyone more deserving of it and I'd hate to see you miss out. By the way, your family will be just fine. God will continue to take care of them just as He's been doing. Nothing is impossible when He's involved. Let Him do what He does best and that is to fix what appears to be irreparable."

Egypt continued to become more a part of her father's family over the weeks and began to enjoy her new living arrangement. She was experiencing things she'd never even thought about before. Poppy and Tara got her into driver's training in anticipation of her going off to college. Once she got her license, a car was even in her future. Her grades were improving though they'd never been terrible. She felt lighter without all of the added pressure. However, she was still concerned about Shae and Corey.

"Poppy, can I talk to you?"

"Sure. What's on your mind?"

"I've been wondering about something."

"Okay. If I can clear it up for you, I will."

"Why don't Shae and Corey come over? I mean, don't you have visitation rights or something?"

"Carolyn and I had several agreements but, because we didn't document it legally, she changed it at will. I'm working on getting those things in place right now. I told you not to concern yourself with these adult issues." Desmond's eyebrows met.

"I didn't tell you this the other day, but Mommy threatened to claim you kidnapped me."

"What? I know your mother gets angry from time to time, but I don't think she would do that. Plus, you're old enough to tell the truth about what happened so she wouldn't have a leg to stand on."

• • •

"I'm not so sure about that. Mommy's doing a lot of stuff I didn't think she would ever do either. She wouldn't even let me come inside to see Corey. She said she wasn't going to allow it anymore since I'm living here with you and Tara. I think she has something to do with Shae barely speaking to me. Everything is falling apart."

"Let me tell you something that might ease your mind a little. I have an attorney and we're working toward resolving all the issues related to the three of you."

"An attorney? Why do you need an attorney?"

"I think it's best to do things this way so everything is done legally. I'm not sure Carolyn and I can come to an agreement on our own especially while she's upset. This way, everything will be documented."

"Mommy doesn't have money for an attorney. That doesn't seem fair." Egypt wrung her hands.

"I'm not trying to take advantage of Carolyn. But at the same time, I don't want her controlling my relationship with you all as she's been doing all of these years. I don't know how it's all going to work out, but I assure you I'll be there for the three of you from now on. As far as Shae is concerned, she'll come around. She's just adjusting to you not being there right now. I'll talk to her and see what she's thinking," Poppy said patting Egypt on the back.

"If you say so. I know Mommy pretty well and she can be vindictive. I don't think she's going to peacefully go along with this."

"It's going to be just fine. You'll see."

Chapter 6

Egypt trudged to the door of her mother's home to pick up Shae for school. She noticed it was dark inside. Egypt wondered if, once again, the bill wasn't paid. She rang the bell and waited for a couple of minutes before she rang the bell again. Finally, her mother came to the door and appeared to be almost sleepwalking.

"What do you want, Egypt?"

"We're here to pick up Shae for school."

"Shae won't need y'all to take her to school anymore. I made other arrangements. You and your Poppy don't have any reason to come here now so I don't expect to see you on at my door again. Understand?"

"I'll tell Poppy. I love you, Mommy. Tell Shae and Corey I love them, too."

"Whatever," Carolyn said as she slammed the door leaving a surprised Egypt standing on the dark doorstep.

"Where's Shae?" Poppy asked when Egypt returned to the truck alone.

"Mommy said she made other arrangements for Shae to get to school so we don't have to pick her up anymore. Then she said she doesn't want me to come back to her house again," Egypt cried.

"I'll look into it and see if there's anything we can do about that," Desmond said as he pulled away from the curb and into traffic.

Chapter 7

"Mr. Lomas, this is Mrs. Riley, the principal at Shae's school."

"Hi, Mrs. Riley. Is everything okay with Shae?"

"No, it's not. That's why I'm calling you. I tried the other number on the contact form and haven't been able to get anyone so I called you."

"Tell me what's going on."

"Shae has eight absences in the last ten days. If she gets any more unexcused absences, we're going to have to take further action. Is there something going on that might be causing her to miss so much school?"

"Shae doesn't live with me so I don't know why she hasn't been in school. Her mother and I aren't getting along right now so that may be playing a part. I haven't been allowed to see Shae myself in a few weeks."

"I see. That may explain some other things that have been going on with Shae."

"What other things?"

"Her teacher reports Shae has been a bit disrespectful lately. She hasn't been doing her homework nor is she fully engaged during the school day. She did much better when Egypt was with her, but we understand that's no longer the case."

"I didn't realize things had gotten so out of hand. Egypt lives with me now. Shae's been upset about that as well. We're all adjusting, but it appears Shae's having a more difficult time than I thought. Regardless of what's going on, there's no excuse for her to be out of line. I'll see what I can do."

"We have staff to deal with these types of concerns. Do you think they could be of assistance?"

"I believe that would be helpful."

"We'll need Shae in school in order to help her. That's the most important thing."

"I'm going to try to contact Carolyn, Shae's mother, and see if I can get things moving in the right direction."

"We appreciate your willingness to help and we'll certainly keep you informed."

"Thank you, Mrs. Riley. We'll keep in touch."

"Take care. Let me know if there's anything else I can do to help."

Desmond hung up the phone and went in search of Tara. He found her in the den reading a book.

"Hey, Des, what's going on? Who was that on the phone?" Tara asked as she walked into the den.

"That was Shae's school."

"What did they want?'

"The principal said Shae hasn't been in school and she's acting out when she is there." Desmond placed his hand to his chin.

"Why hasn't she been going to school?" Tara asked.

"I don't know, but I'm sure Carolyn has her reasons."

"What reason could she have?"

"With Egypt not being there to take care of everything, Carolyn has to step up. Apparently, she's either unable or unwilling to handle things. Carolyn is not doing her job as a mother."

"Poppy?" Egypt said from the hall outside of the den.

"Hey, Egypt."

"I heard what you said about Shae."

"Don't concern yourself Egypt. It's going to be all right."

"But you keep saying that and things are getting worse."

"I know that's what it looks like, but it's usually darkest before dawn."

"I'm beginning to wonder if it's really going to work out."

"I promise it will. I know I've said that before, but it's true. Just give it a little more time."

"It doesn't sound like we have any more time. Shae's missing a lot of school and she's acting up too. All of this is because I didn't keep my mouth shut and just do what needed to be done." Egypt paced in the hall.

"Don't go blaming yourself again. This has nothing to do with you."

"It does, Poppy. You know it and so do I. I've been thinking that I should just try to go back home. That way, I'll know Shae and Corey are okay." Resigned, Egypt turned to walk away.

Desmond's hands gripped Egypt's shoulders. "Absolutely not. You are staying here, finishing high school, taking that scholarship and going to college. You are going to become the journalist you've always wanted to be. We are not having this discussion again."

"But at what expense, Poppy? Mommy's mad at me. Shae's not doing well. I don't even know what's happening with Corey. I feel like I've already lost a lot. I just don't know if it's worth it. With all due respect, this is my decision. I'm going to my room."

"Let me ask you something, Egypt."

"Okay."

"Did it ever cross your mind that achieving your dream isn't just for you? I think it's important for Corey and Shae to see you do it. You are an example for them. If you give up on your dreams, you're telling them it's okay for them to do the same. Think about that while you're making your decision."

Chapter 8

"May I speak to Poppy, please?" a panicked Shae asked Tara when she answered the phone.

"Shae?"

"Yes. Can you please get my daddy?" Shae screamed.

"Sure, Shae. Just a moment."

Tara ran through the house looking for Desmond. It sounded like there was some sort of emergency and she needed to find him quickly. Shae never called, especially since Egypt had left home, so that made Tara move even faster.

"Des, where are you?"

"I'm right here. What's going on?" Desmond said as Tara fell into him as he came out of his office.

"Shae's on the phone and she sounds really upset. She asked to speak to you."

Tara pushed the phone into Desmond's hand. Egypt, hearing the commotion, came out of her room to see what was happening as well. The three of them stood in the hall as Shae explained her reason for calling.

"Shae, hey baby, is everything all right?" Desmond said.

"Poppy, I know I'm not supposed to call you. I'm not supposed to tell anybody about what goes on in this house. But, Mommy's real sick and I don't know what to do."

"What do you mean she's sick?"

"I'm not supposed to say," Shae said.

"You have to tell me so I can help."

"She left me and Corey here last night and when she came back this morning she was sick. Corey is screaming and I don't know what's wrong with him either."

"You were home alone last night with Corey?"

"Mommy said I'm a big girl now and I can take care of myself and Corey. I don't even have to go to school anymore. I have to be responsible. Did I do a good job, Poppy?"

"Yes, you did, honey. You did a good job. I'm going to come over there to see what's wrong with Mommy and Corey. When I get there, I want you to let me in, okay? Don't open the door for anybody else. Can you do that for Poppy?"

"Yes, hurry up though because Mommy can't stay awake and Corey's screaming is about to drive me crazy."

"I'm coming right now."

"I'm coming with you, Des. Egypt, do you mind staying here with the kids?"

"No, I'm going," Egypt stated firmly.

"Tara, I don't think you should go," Desmond said. "I don't want to make Carolyn any angrier than she is. Egypt, let's go."

"Call me if you need me. I'll be right by the phone," Tara assured him.

Chapter 9

Desmond and Egypt slowly walked to the front door of Carolyn's home. They could hear Corey's cries even from the street. They knocked on the door unsure of what to expect. The door swung open revealing Shae's tear-streaked face. She led them to where Carolyn was lying. Her mouth was hanging open and her clothing appeared as though she'd been rolling around in mud.

"Mommy, what's wrong with you?"

"What are you doing here?" Carolyn asked. Then noticing Desmond, she added, "With him?"

"Shae said you were sick."

"I'm fine. I don't know what it is about you girls. You just can't keep your mouth shut when it comes to Poppy and my business," Carolyn said as she rolled over onto her back.

"You don't look fine," Desmond said.

"I might've been a little inebriated last night. That's all. No big deal." She rose, wiping the remains of drool from the side of her face.

"Why did you leave Shae and Corey here alone? And why hasn't Shae been going to school?" Desmond inquired.

"Who told you that?"

"It doesn't matter. I'm still waiting for an answer."

"Shae is staying home to do the job your little Egypt didn't want to do. She doesn't have time for school." Carolyn stated with upturned lips.

"She has to go to school. Her education is important for her future, Carolyn. Can't you see that?"

"Why is everyone so concerned about the future? No one's concerned about my future."

"This isn't about you. This should be about our children."

"You can leave now that you see everything is okay," Carolyn said attempting to smooth her hair down.

"No, I'm not just leaving Shae and Corey here. I don't think they're safe. I'm taking them with me," Desmond declared.

"No, you're not!" Carolyn pushed Desmond toward the exit but Desmond was too strong.

"I don't care what you say, Carolyn. Enough is enough. These kids have been through more than they should have and I blame myself for it as much as I do you."

"You are not leaving here with my kids. If I have to, I'll call the police. You already left here with Egypt. I'm not just going to stand by and let you leave with the others."

"I guess you'll have to call the police because I am taking them."

"Poppy, what if I stay? I'll take care of everything. That way no one will get in trouble, you won't have to go to court, and things can get back to normal."

"We've already discussed this and I recall telling you we weren't discussing it again. Go help get Shae and Corey ready to go."

Egypt reluctantly went to gather some belongings for Corey and Shae. She found Corey whimpering in his bed. He'd taken off a diaper that looked as though he'd been wearing it for days. She went to the bathroom to get a washcloth to clean him up as her parents continued to argue. She returned and laid Corey down on the bed and found an extreme case of diaper rash. No wonder he was screaming so much. She laid out some diapers and the few

* * *

pieces of clothing he had, considering he didn't go out much. She instructed Shae to get some things together as well. She found a couple of plastic bags in the kitchen for her siblings' belongings.

When the trio returned to the living room, they found their parents still arguing so much that neither noticed their children in the room.

"We're ready," Egypt said loudly so Desmond and Carolyn could hear her.

***

Tara opened the door to find her husband and three stepchildren looking as though they'd been through a major battle.

"Come on in, kids. I've been waiting for you. Are you hungry?"

"No. I want to go home," Shae sternly responded with crossed arms and lips poked out.

"I bet you'll be hungry when you hear what I have for you."

"What do you have?"

"I heard you like pizza so I ordered some for us to have tonight."

Shae reconsidered. "Well, maybe I'll have a little. But right after that Poppy's going to take me home."

Everyone laughed as they entered the eat-in kitchen and began fixing plates filled with pizza, salad and bread sticks. Glasses and cups held grape Kool-Aid to drink. Afterwards, they watched a movie in the spacious family room. Corey immediately fell asleep as Shae intently watched the movie along with her siblings. Desmond and Tara supervised the activities as they relaxed from the eventful evening. Egypt observed Corey looking so peaceful and Shae who looked as content as she ever had. Egypt realized she enjoyed not having the job of juggling all she'd been handling for so long. She recognized, in her mind, that Shae and Corey weren't her responsibility. However, she couldn't just flip the switch in her heart and not feel they were her charges. For now, they were safe at her father's house. Egypt felt everything was lining up to allow her to take the scholarship and head off to college. For the first time in a long time, she felt upbeat about her life.

The doorbell rang.

"Were you expecting someone?" Desmond asked Tara.

"No. I thought it must be someone here to see you."

"I don't think so. I'll be right here when you get back from answering the door."

"You're really going to send me to the door in the dark of night?" Tara shook her head.

"When you put it that way, I guess that wouldn't be right."

Arriving at the door, Desmond questioned, "Who's there?"

"You better open that door right now. I'm here to get my kids."

"Carolyn, I am not opening this door for you tonight. We already talked about this. Get yourself together and we'll talk."

"Oh yes, you are going to open the door tonight. Look out your window, peephole or whatever you rich people use to see who's on their property."

Desmond, wishing he'd thought of that before he went to the door, utilized the surveillance camera in the highest corner of his multi-story porch for just that purpose. When he did, he realized he would have to open the door. Two police officers flanked Carolyn who was wearing a huge smile on her face and waving as though she was posing for pictures.

"Officers, what can I do for you?"

"Sir, we received a call from the children's mother reporting a case of parental kidnapping. We're here to take the children."

"These children are mine too and I did not kidnap them."

"This lady here says you took the children without her permission. Whether you're the father or not, that can be viewed as kidnapping."

"Did she tell you why I removed the children from her home?"

"No, sir. She did not."

"She left the two youngest alone last night so she could go out. She came home intoxicated from God only knows what. My daughter called me panicking because she was scared. Shae hasn't been going to school. I did what I thought was best for Shae and Corey."

"Officer, arrest him for lying under oath or something."

"Ma'am, did you leave the children unsupervised?"

"No, I would never leave my precious children like that."

"What's going on?" Tara asked as she approached the foyer with Egypt right behind her.

"Mommy, what are you doing here?" Egypt stepped forward.

"Is this one of your minor children ma'am?" The police asked.

Carolyn grinned. "Yes, it is."

"What are you doing?" Egypt inquired.

"I'm here to get my kids."

"Poppy, can she do that?"

• • •

"I'm not sure. I'm going to get my lawyer on the phone."

"We don't have time for your little lawyer to weigh in on this. Where are Corey and Shae?" Carolyn stepped past the police, entering the home.

She walked through the foyer looking around the house for her two younger children. She passed the den and the formal dining room before Tara brought her tour to a halt.

"I'll thank you to stay on the porch," Tara demanded.

"Oh, I'll thank you not to talk to me and I'll go wherever I want," Carolyn continued looking for Shae and Corey.

"Miss, she's asked you not to trespass. I suggest you don't do so," the policeman warned.

Carolyn reluctantly changed direction and stepped back outside of the house. Desmond returned after attempting to contact his attorney.

"I'm going to release the children to you since I couldn't reach my lawyer. But, Carolyn, you need to know this isn't over. I would be less of a father if I didn't attempt to insure my children's security. Tara, go get Corey and Shae. Egypt, go get their things."

"Poppy, no!"

* * *

Egypt left the foyer to gather Shae and Corey's belongings. She thought about all that had transpired over the past few weeks. Nothing could have prepared her for this.

As she reflected on Grandma Peete's words from years ago, she never knew how much of a fight it would be. The battle was indeed intense. Though Egypt knew what she wanted to do, she also had to acknowledge what she might need to do.

Success was at hand yet so far away. All she had to do was take the scholarship as her father and teacher suggested and she would be on her way to success as she defined it.

How could she focus with everything in such upheaval? How could she leave? After all, there was no way to know how this would be resolved. How long it would take was also a big question mark.

This was going to be a battle to the death if her mother had anything to do with it. Even with Poppy fighting for their well-being, Egypt was convinced Corey and Shae's welfare would be secondary to Carolyn's need to have "a life."

What about Egypt's right to live her life? Egypt went to her bedroom for a moment. Her bedroom. What a novel concept. She didn't have to share a room with her two siblings. If nothing else changed, this alone made it all worth it. She knelt down on the side of her bed and began to pray. She needed to make a decision regarding the scholarship and let Mrs. Matlin know tomorrow. She also needed to decide whether to leave with her mother tonight to care for her younger siblings. After her period of prayer, Egypt knew what her decision would be. Now she just had to let everyone else in on it.

* * *

Chapter 10

"All I can tell you, Desmond, is that I got a call from Carolyn's lawyer asking for this last-minute meeting. They only gave us an hour to get here. I don't know what that's about," Attorney Lawson, Desmond's friend, stated as he led Desmond and Egypt into the law office.

"So, nobody gave you a clue what's going on?" Desmond asked.

"No, they didn't," Attorney Lawson replied. "This is highly unusual though, Des. I'm uneasy because I don't know what to expect."

The three arrived at the receptionist's desk out of breath. Arriving at the impromptu appointment on time required brisk movement to achieve. The receptionist directed them to a conference room down the hall. Attorney Lawson followed by Desmond and Egypt entered the room. Egypt saw her mother and her lawyer already in place.

"I'm glad you were able to come on such short notice," Carolyn's lawyer stated, as everyone took a seat.

"Thank you. What is this meeting about?" Attorney Lawson asked.

"My client has something she would like to say." Carolyn's attorney motioned for his client to speak.

"I'm going to let you have the kids, Desmond," Carolyn conceded.

"Just like that? I have a hard time believing that," Desmond said.

"Believe it."

"Why? What's changed?" Desmond leaned forward.

"Nothing has changed," Carolyn said.

"Are you serious?" Desmond wondered.

"Yes, I'm serious. If you keep questioning me, we can continue to drag this out."

"I don't want that. We'll need this in writing of course."

"That's already done."

Desmond and Attorney Lawson looked over the documents Carolyn's lawyer slid across the table. Desmond smiled.

"You might think you won, but I'm the real winner."

* * *

"This wasn't a contest. Shae and Corey's well-being was at stake here," Poppy explained.

"I beg to differ, Poppy. I haven't wanted to be a mother to these kids for a long time. Now, I don't even have to fake the funk anymore. You got them and I'm okay with that. I can get on with my life now," Carolyn confessed.

"That's so sad," Desmond lamented.

"It's not really," Carolyn said. "Everybody's so worried about Egypt being able to pursue her dreams. She isn't the only one who has dreams. I have dreams too and now, I have the freedom to live them."

"What's your dream, Carolyn?"

"To be free of these kids. That's my dream."

"Tara and I could've taken the kids a long time ago, but you refused to cooperate."

"I've been fighting with you just for the fun of making you miserable. The problem was I was hurting myself too. I feel like someone lifted a couple of loads off me. Everybody gets what they want. Oh, I'm sorry. Egypt, I guess you won't get to take that scholarship. Moving back in with me and the kids wasn't the best decision. Don't worry though. You can still get state aid just like women in my family have always done," Carolyn teased.

"You're wrong, Mommy. I accepted that scholarship. I just didn't tell you. I knew you wouldn't let me stay in your house and watch Shae and Corey if I told you that. I won't be going down to get on the state. I'm making a new tradition for our family. We can go to school if we want."

"You sneaky little … you know what? I can't even knock you for that. You got sneaky from me," Carolyn said while wagging her finger.

"Speaking of sneaky, what did you do with the money Poppy was giving you?" Egypt inquired.

"Money?"

"Yeah, Carolyn. You know. The money you said I wasn't giving you to help you out with the kids."

"Oh, that money. It was so much fun making you look bad. These kids were 'Poppy' crazy until I told them you weren't so crazy about them." Carolyn chuckled.

"Well, what happened to the money?" Desmond asked.

"I was saving that for my afterlife," Carolyn responded seriously.

"You might not have gone to church much, Carolyn, but I think you know money won't do you much good after you die," Desmond joked.

"I do know that. However, that's not the afterlife I'm talking about," Carolyn said.

"I didn't know there was another one," Poppy stated.

"Whatever," Carolyn yelled.

"Well, I didn't," Poppy said.

"See, I had a premonition this day would come. I didn't know it would take this long, but I did know it would happen eventually. Every day I would get up and wonder if that would be the day you would finally take your kids off my hands. I took that money and put most of it away for my afterlife. I partied with the rest of it. A girl's got to have some fun, you know."

"We struggled so you could have money for your afterlife? What is this afterlife you keep talking about?" Egypt wondered.

"I was trying to tell you but you interrupted me. You would think with all that education, you would know better. Anyway, it was to support my lifestyle after you, Shae, and Corey got out of my house. I saved it for my life after kids. Thanks to your Poppy taking so long, I have enough to live very well for quite a while.

My future is very bright." Carolyn laughed. "Thanks, Poppy!" Carolyn put her sunglasses on, turned, and walked out of her lawyer's office suite a free woman. Her job was complete.

"Carolyn, don't leave the kids like this! Do you know what it'll do to them if you abandon them?" Desmond said as he moved toward her.

Egypt, grabbing her father's arm, stated, "Let her go, Poppy. She obviously doesn't want to be a mother and we can't make her be one."

Egypt reached inside her purse, pulled her sunglasses out and placed them on her face.

"What is it with you, your mother and these sunglasses?" Poppy asked.

"She's not the only one that needs sunglasses heading into her future," Egypt responded and lead her father and lawyer out of the office.

Questions for Reflection

Do you think Egypt had a responsibility to give up her dream and care for her siblings?

What do you think was at the root of Carolyn's treatment of Egypt?

Does Desmond bear some responsibility for what was occurring with Egypt, Shae and Corey? Should he have been more aggressive in seeking to be a part of his children's lives?

Do you think Carolyn is still in love with Desmond?

Was Carolyn within her rights to expect Egypt to participate in Shae and Corey's upbringing to the extent she did?

Have you ever carried responsibility that belonged to someone else? What effect did it have on you? Do you still carry it? Are you willing to release it to God?

Do you think there are those that depend on you to reach your dream? Do you believe that God gives us dreams that, when achieved, will benefit someone else?

Do you believe we should delay pursuing our God-given dreams? Can you think of a valid reason why you should/would delay the pursuit of your dream?

Do you believe our dreams align with God's purpose for our lives?

What dreams do you believe God has given you that you have delayed or given up on pursuing? What was the reason for your decision? Identify what is holding you back.

Choose to revive those dreams. List each one then develop a plan to realize at least one from your list. What attitudes, relationships or habits do you need to adjust in order to attain your goal? Include those things in your plan.

Twice Bitten

Chapter 1

Chriselle labored up the stairs. She walked past a few empty bedrooms and a full bathroom to the last room on the left. It was her daughter Leslie's bedroom. She entered the room with its soft orange sorbet colored walls, wood floors, white bedroom furniture and orange and fuchsia floral comforter. Sitting in the cantaloupe-colored chair near the window, Chriselle began to think about Leslie and Bryce's wedding earlier that day.

"I now pronounce you man and wife. You may kiss the bride."

Chriselle reminisced about her daughter's wedding while pulling a tissue from the box sitting on the side table. Those words were life changing. They changed Chriselle's life when she said them over thirty years ago, and they changed her child's life today. Her last child, Leslie, was now officially someone's wife, complete with a change of address form and a moving van.

Chriselle remembered all those years ago when she said those same vows. She had dreams and thoughts about what her life would be like as a Mrs. She just didn't know how big those dreams were at the time.

The look of love in the eyes of Leslie and her new husband, Bryce, said it all. Their deep love and commitment was evident today. No one and nothing in the world could come between them today. Their minds couldn't even comprehend that anything in life could be better. However, sometimes things indeed change and you find out that "forever" means something much shorter.

The traditional wedding vows include a promise to stay together until death. Chriselle wondered if anything other than physical death counted. She felt like she died as a person, as a woman. All those years of raising children, taking care of a house, and over thirty years of being a wife caused her to forget what her life was like beforehand.

Gazing out of the nearby window overlooking the family's swimming pool, Chriselle realized Leslie wouldn't be home making blueberry pancakes for breakfast tomorrow morning. She wouldn't be sitting with Chriselle in the adult Sunday school class as she'd been doing since she became old enough to join her. Instead, she'd be in some exotic location enjoying her first days of marriage not even thinking about the fact Chriselle felt lost.

. . .

Chriselle moved to the bed and stretched her body across it, inhaling the residual signature scent of her youngest daughter. Her thoughts shifted to the nights she sat in this bed with Leslie and read Bible stories. She recalled kneeling on this very floor with her to pray. The memory of Leslie announcing her engagement came to mind. That was when Chriselle felt she'd lost her purpose.

All of her children— three sons and two daughters—had gone on with their lives. How dare they do that? They must have forgotten everything she'd done for them. She wiped runny noses, spent more time in the emergency room than she cared to remember, attempted to mend broken hearts, kept them clean and presentable, and introduced them to Jesus Christ. And what did she get in return? She got an empty house. And she found herself resentful of it. Yes, they often came to visit and brought their spouses and children. Still, Chriselle was overcome by emotional and physical emptiness.

Drew, Chriselle's husband, came into the room just as she crushed her tissue and added it to the pile already established on the bed. She didn't want him to see her like this. She didn't want him to know about her pain. After looking into his eyes, she realized he already knew this pain almost as intimately as she did. He held her in his arms and stroked her hair, his best effort at comforting her. She didn't think he could feel it as deeply as she did. He had a life. She'd been a housewife and mother all these years. Now that the demands were different, Chriselle didn't know what to do with herself. Surrounded by Drew's arms, Chriselle couldn't remember the last time she felt the spark she and Drew once shared. She realized she didn't even feel a tingle. What happened to me? What happened to us?

Chapter 2

"Baby, let's go do something fun today," Chriselle said to Drew.

"What do you want to do?" he responded, pulling on a pair of jean shorts in the couple's master walk-in closet.

"I don't know; something out of the ordinary."

"Well, if you come up with something, maybe we'll do it."

"Why don't you plan something for us to do? I would really like that," Chriselle said lightly touching Drew's arm.

"You're the one who wants to do something, so you plan it. I'm sure you already have something in mind," Drew said as he pulled on a T-shirt and grabbed his tennis shoes.

"Actually, I do. The play I told you I wanted to see is opening tonight. Let's go see if we can get tickets."

"I have some yard work I have to do and then, if I have time, I'm going to wash the cars. So you go get the tickets and let me know what time I need to be ready to go."

Chriselle pouted. "It's no fun if you just send me to do all the legwork by myself. I want you to be excited about it and get involved with planning our special evening. I think we should make a reservation at that new soul food restaurant by the theater, too. That'll be really nice."

"I told you I have other things to do this morning."

"Why can't you do the lawn later? You can even do it tomorrow."

"I want to go ahead and get it done this morning. I'll be sitting right here waiting on you when you get back."

"It would mean a lot to me if you would participate in planning this date."

"Please let me take care of the yard, and I'll make it up to you later," Drew promised.

***

Chriselle left the house with a new level of disappointment. As she drove toward the theater, she realized how much she desired her husband to be just as invested in them going out and having fun and in changing the monotony of their lives as she was. Drew never seemed to want to do anything outside of their normal routine. Every day, Drew got up at 3:30 a.m. to get ready for work. Chriselle got up along with him to prepare a light breakfast, fill his to-go cup with coffee, kiss him lightly on the lips and then back to bed. Every morning when she got up for the second time, she had her devotional time with God—then she waited. She waited until she got an idea of what to do with the rest of her day. She didn't have to prepare dinner until six o'clock. The house was neat and tidy since no one was there except her all day. Oprah signed-off for the last time, so she didn't even have that to look forward to. The silence was deafening and the boredom was crippling. Drew came home about six thirty, kissed Chriselle hello, ate dinner, told her about his day and then knocked out in front of the television. Chriselle watched him sleep until nine o'clock when she woke him to go to bed. Chriselle and Drew seemed to blink and then the alarm woke them up to start the whole process over again. What a life! Watching her children spread their wings and live their lives their own way inspired Chriselle to want to do the same. Just to get out and do some things she'd always wanted to do. The problem was Drew had settled into a routine.

Regardless, Drew was a great husband and an even better father. He did whatever was necessary to provide for the wants and needs of five offspring and a wife. The family lived in a beautiful custom-built five-bedroom house. They traveled all over the United States and even to other parts of the world as a family. Each of their children and grandchildren, while not perfect, was a tremendous source of pride. Drew and Chriselle also remained healthy, allowing them to still move about and live their lives as they desired. God was definitely good to them.

When Chriselle first met Drew, she was studying counseling. Drew was on a basketball scholarship at the same university studying architecture. He was handsome and very talented. She observed him both on the court as well as off the court at parties and other social events. He was a social animal. She loved that about him. He mingled with ease. Eventually they met and began dating. Then the unexpected happened, Drew lost his scholarship. All that social activity caught up with him and his lack of studying caused his grades to drop below the acceptable level. His family was unable to finance the rest of his education so he had to drop out. He found a job in the local factory where he worked until this very day. He intended to return to finish his degree program but never did. That didn't change her love for him. He was her soul mate.

After Chriselle's graduation, they got married. She worked up until the time their first child was born. From that point on, Drew was the sole provider. He never once complained when he had to pick up additional work for one reason or another. He ate whatever she put before him and not once did he point out when she burned the biscuits or the meat was tough. He never belittled the fact she didn't work outside of the home. When she didn't lose weight after each child she bore, he cherished her just the same.

Yet she found herself wanting him to make a little more effort. It seemed he retired, retired from taking care of the two of them in ways other than meeting their basic physical needs.

***

When she returned, as expected, Drew was asleep in front of the TV. She went to her retreat room and worked on one of her many projects. Drew woke up a couple hours later and jumped in the shower to get ready. While she looked through her jewelry box to choose suitable accessories for her ensemble, Drew came up behind her and fastened a diamond-encrusted cross necklace around her neck.

"This is for you my dear. I noticed you admiring this piece while we were in the jewelry store picking up my watch." Drew moved in front of Chriselle to view the new accessory.

"Drew! When? What? I can't believe it. It's gorgeous." Chriselle smiled and pulled back her collar to see the jewelry a little better.

"Don't think I haven't noticed you being a little down since Leslie left. I just want you to know you're still my girl."

"But how long have you had this?"

"I put it in layaway waiting for the perfect opportunity to give it to you. When you went downtown to buy the tickets, I rushed over there and picked it up for tonight."

"You amaze me. Just when I think I have you figured out, you turn around and surprise me. Thank you. It's perfect. You are so good to me. Thank you, baby."

"This is just a token of my appreciation for the best wife and mother I know. We'll always need you no matter what. Don't ever underestimate your value." Drew hugged his wife, reinforcing his words.

***

"Chriselle, if you could do whatever you wanted to do, what would you do now that the children have all moved on with their lives?" Drew challenged his wife after they placed their meal orders.

Chriselle waited a moment as she thought about her answer.

• • •

"Well, I've been thinking about that since Leslie got married. I didn't realize how much I depended on the children to fill my life. Now that they're all gone, I do need something else to do."

"I know you miss them, but, it's our time now. You said you've been thinking. Do you have any ideas?"

"I'm considering resuming my career. What do you think about that?"

Drew frowned. "Honey, I thought you would want to do something a little more fun or maybe explore some interest you haven't had the opportunity to before. Why do you want to go back to a job?" Drew said, as the server placed their entrees in front of them.

"I just thought I might want to pick up where I left off. I put my career on hold when we started our family. Don't get me wrong, I enjoyed being a stay-at-home mom and I wouldn't have it any other way. I just feel like there's a bit of unfinished business there."

They held hands as Drew blessed their food.

"I would like for you to stay home and enjoy yourself. I'm retiring soon, and I'd like us to do some traveling among other things. We've discussed relocating a couple of times, too. We'll have to push those plans out if you're working. I think we've both worked hard all these years so it's our time. I can just see us living on a nice little lake somewhere, coasting in our pontoon boat or fishing from the shore."

Chriselle thought about what Drew said. It made a lot of sense. All but the pontoon boat, that is. For some reason, it seemed like it still wasn't enough. Obviously, his idea of fun did not mirror hers. She wanted to travel to exotic locations and dance the night away. The long-desired trip to Paris and a safari in Africa came to mind. Things like that were more her cup of tea.

Wielding her knife and fork to cut her chicken, she said, "I feel like there's a hole that needs filling. I do hear what you're saying as well. I think I lost myself. I'll pray about it some more."

"That's exactly what you should do. Let's talk about it again before you make a final decision on that."

. . .

Chapter 3

Months later, Chriselle began a new job working in the advising office at the local community college. Drew was okay with her working, with the understanding they would re-evaluate things once he retired. It gave Chriselle a much-needed meaningful outlet, and Drew's plans for them wouldn't be restricted once he entered into retirement.

After her last appointment for the week, Chriselle cleared her desk, putting away paperwork that hadn't found its way home during the day. She sat and picked up her work journal to download all the concerns from the day. As she completed her journal entry, she noticed someone standing in the doorway of her office. She looked up prepared to tell the person they would have to return Monday but found a familiar smiling face.

"Chriselle Addison. It is you. When I saw the name Chriselle in the new hires email, I thought it might be you, but the last name threw me. I had to come by to see if it was you."

"Well, I'll be. Jordan Franklin. How are you? It's been a long time." Chriselle rose from her chair and went to hug the man. "Come on in and have a seat." Jordan settled into one of the upholstered chairs offered by Chriselle. "So, do you work in this department, too?"

"Yes, I do. I've been here for over fifteen years. What have you been doing with yourself?"

"I've been a housewife. My last child just got married so I decided to resume my career. What about you?"

"Well, I've been married and divorced."

"Oh, I'm so sorry to hear that," Chriselle lamented.

"It took a while to heal. Then I realized it was for the best. Are you still married, Chriselle?"

"Yes, I am."

"Oh. That's nice." Jordan looked away.

"What does that mean?"

"You know I haven't forgotten about us even after all this time. When I found out you might be working here I thought maybe...it doesn't matter what I thought." He said waving off the thought.

"Jordan, I don't know what to say."

"There's nothing left to say. I'll see you around. I know you'll do well in your new job. Let me know if I can be of help." Jordan stood up from the seat and left the office.

Chriselle continued clearing her desk and put things in place in anticipation of the next week. She was speechless. She couldn't believe the coincidence that Jordan was working in the same department as her. His appearance in her office totally caught her off guard. It was obvious he was still harboring some feelings for her. She hoped their past relationship wouldn't pose a problem in the workplace.

Chapter 4

"How was work today?" Drew asked his wife as she entered the couple's home.

"It was tiring but fulfilling. Those young people really need a lot of direction," Chriselle responded, putting her things away for the weekend. "I'm ready to change out of these clothes and into some sweats."

"You go ahead and I'll finish dinner." Drew kissed his wife on the forehead and returned to the kitchen to turn the steaks. He removed the baked potatoes from the double oven, cut them open, buttered them, and placed one on each plate. He retrieved the tossed salad from the refrigerator and placed a serving in each of two bowls. He prepared the salad and baked potato fixings for the dining room table. Drew carefully checked the steaks and decided they were at their desired doneness. Chriselle returned to the kitchen and began helping Drew get everything on the table. She poured the sparkling beverage her husband had chilled for the evening into wine glasses and positioned fruit slices on the rims for a decorative touch. With everything done, the couple entered the dining room. Drew said the blessing over the meal and the two ate.

Drew noticed Chriselle was quieter than normal. She seemed distracted. This concerned him. His desire was for her to be ecstatic, if possible. If he sensed she wasn't, he was determined to change it as swiftly as he could.

"What's wrong? Did something happen at work?" Drew asked, touching his wife's hand.

"I ran into an old friend today."

"I would think you'd be happy about that. Who was it? Could you pass the pepper?"

"Someone I know from high school," Chriselle said as she slid the pepper grinder across the table.

"O-kay," Drew said drawing out each syllable of the word. "Care to elaborate?" He placed his utensils on the side of his plate and focused on Chriselle.

"I feel bad about how we left things the last time we talked. It wasn't good."

"Look, sometimes things happen that way. Some friendships have an expiration date and once you get past that time, it ends for some reason. It's no one's fault. It just happens."

"Somehow, I think I may be directly responsible in this case."

Drew discerned the sorrow on his wife's face. "I don't know the details, but maybe an apology would help. Who knows, you might be able to reclaim the friendship."

Chriselle thought for a couple of minutes about Drew's suggestion. Thinking back, she probably didn't apologize. Maybe, Drew was right. An apology certainly couldn't hurt and maybe in this case it could even help. After all, she had to work with Jordan and didn't want the obvious awkwardness to exist between them.

"I think that's the best approach. I'll apologize and see what happens from there." Chriselle instantly felt better and perked up. "What are we doing this weekend?"

Chapter 5

Chriselle followed the student out of her office and to the front desk to gather some necessary materials for him. She also wanted to insure they scheduled a follow-up appointment. Afterwards, Chriselle headed back to her office. Just as she rounded the corner, she saw Jordan peeking into her office as if to look for her in the far corners of the space.

"Are you looking for someone?" Chriselle asked, startling Jordan.

"I was just stopping by to say hello."

"I need to talk to you anyway. Can you come in for a minute?"

"I have a better idea. Can you take a break?"

"Not really. I have to eat at my desk today."

"Okay." Jordan stepped aside, allowing Chriselle to enter first. Once inside, Chriselle gestured toward a worktable in the corner of her office. Each took a seat at the worktable.

Chriselle laced her fingers together on top of the table before she spoke. "Jordan, let me get right to the point. I feel like there might be some lingering tension between the two of us because of our past."

"What makes you think that?" Jordan countered, leaning back in his chair.

"I sense it. Don't you?"

"Actually, I don't. I'm not sure what you're sensing, but I don't have anything against you. You made your decision and I accepted it."

"You're not angry with me?"

"I used to be, but not now. Maybe you feel guilty because of what you did and want to blame it on me."

"Well, I asked you to come in so I could say I'm sorry about my part in what happened between us."

"All right. I accept your apology, but that doesn't change how I feel," Jordan calmly stated.

Chriselle sat at her desk with her mouth gaping. As Jordan turned to leave, she repeated the conversation over in her head, trying to figure out what just happened.

Chapter 6

Chriselle and Drew drove up to the park for the college's faculty and staff appreciation gathering. The tree-lined dirt road was beautiful, considering the changing colors of the fall foliage. Once they came into the clearing, they followed the signs directing them to the parking area for the event. She'd wanted Drew to come so badly she agreed to drive separately, since Drew had to leave and go in to work. They parked and walked towards the tent reserved for the gathering, greeting co-workers along the way. Chriselle gravitated towards the people she worked most closely with to introduce her husband before he had to leave. After those initial introductions, they headed to the food area.

"Hi, Chriselle. I'm glad you made it," Jordan said, greeting Chriselle while biting down on a hot dog.

"Hi, Jordan. How long have you been here?" she responded, noticing her stomach turning flips over this man just because he showed up apparently.

"I've been here about an hour or so. Are you here by yourself?"

"No, my husband is over there." She pointed at Drew getting fish from the grill.

"Oh."

"Why do you keep saying 'oh' whenever I mention my husband?"

"What do you expect me to say?"

"I guess I don't know," Chriselle thought about it.

"Well, I'm going to see what I can get into. I'll see you around," Jordan said, as he turned to walk away from Chriselle as Drew returned.

"Who was that, baby?" Drew asked, regarding the man he saw talking to his wife.

"That's one of my new co-workers who happens to be an old friend as well," Chriselle said with a faraway look.

"What kind of old friend?" Drew wondered aloud.

"He used to be my boyfriend in high school."

"Really? Were you two serious?"

"As serious as two seventeen-year-olds could be."

***

Drew heard what his wife said but felt something wasn't quite right about Chriselle's explanation. He remembered a recent conversation where Chriselle mentioned a high school classmate she was down about. Drew wondered if this was whom she was referring to. The two walked around the grounds getting to know Chriselle's coworkers. Eventually, Chriselle and Drew walked into a group of people talking which included Jordan. Once they joined the conversation, Jordan moved away toward another group that was playing spades. Chriselle noticed his unwillingness to be around her and wondered if the awkwardness would ever leave. What happened between them happened a long time ago and she wondered why he was still reacting as though it just happened yesterday.

"I have to go. I'll see you at home a little later," Drew said, interrupting Chriselle's thoughts.

"Can't you stay a while longer?" Chriselle begged.

"The sooner I get there, the sooner I'll be home. Besides, you're here enjoying the party anyway. You won't even miss me," Drew said, pulling Chriselle into a casual embrace.

"I will miss you, but that's okay. I know you have to go. I'll see you later on tonight."

Drew hugged his wife and turned to leave the area. He looked back toward the group and noticed Chriselle walking in the general direction of her former boyfriend. Something about this turn of events bothered him, but he wasn't sure exactly why. He changed his direction once more to head to his car. He got in and left. He decided to see what he could do about cutting his shift a little so he could come back. Chriselle seemed as though she really wanted him to be there with her and he wanted to oblige her.

***

Chriselle approached the crowd gathered around a lively card game. She stood next to Jordan as everyone shouted their response to what was happening at the table. When the game was over and the pair that lost the round got up, the search began for two new players to take on the winners. Finally, Jordan volunteered, and Chriselle decided to play along with him as his partner.

"I haven't played in so long. It looks like fun," Chriselle excitedly stated.

"Well, don't sit down if you can't play now. I play to win." Jordan laughed.

"You just take care of yourself. I know what I'm doing!"

Chriselle love the bantering back and forth that a good game of spades brought on. This was what she'd been missing in her life. Fun. The fact that she and Jordan were winning made it much more enjoyable. She couldn't remember the last time she laughed so much. Two hours later, Jordan and Chriselle voluntarily gave up their seats. They walked away from the table laughing and commenting about the way they operated as a team.

"So, I guess I must have done okay," Chriselle joked.

"I forget how good you are at spades," Jordan commented.

"We used to play all the time. I'm surprised you doubted me."

"You have to admit a lot has happened that caused me to doubt you," Jordan said, bringing the conversation to a serious level.

Chriselle stopped and looked deeply into Jordan's eyes. They revealed the pain she'd caused all those years ago. Tonight, she felt alive once again, and Jordan was a direct cause of that. Old feelings were bubbling up inside of her. It was not a good thing for a married woman to experience these feelings when they involved a man other than her husband. Somehow, feelings don't always act as expected, and Chriselle was quickly realizing that. She knew what he was referring to and he was correct. She had caused him to doubt her. She did probably owe him an explanation, though that wouldn't change anything. Their relationship ended so long ago and she felt he should've been over it. Apparently, that wasn't the case. Chriselle didn't know how to respond to Jordan continuously bringing up their history. She felt she should acknowledge Jordan's feelings. But how?

"Well, this was certainly a day to remember," she commented.

"Oh, okay. You're just going to ignore what I said."

"What do you want me to say? It's done and over with."

"Is it?" Jordan questioned.

Jordan grabbed Chriselle by the waist and pulled her close. She didn't resist, and that did not escape the eyes of an observer standing not far away.

***

Drew left work early to surprise his wife by coming back to the gathering. He didn't expect to find her there spending so much time with Jordan. He watched for a while as the two of them laughed and talked trash at the card table. He saw their interaction as they spoke. Drew wasn't a naturally jealous man so the feeling he was experiencing was unusual for him. Deciding he wasn't interested in creating a scene and believing in the security of his marriage, Drew left the park and headed home to wait for his wife there.

Chapter 7

Chriselle returned to work the following Monday still enjoying the high from the outing over the weekend. She thoroughly enjoyed her time with Jordan playing cards. The chemistry between them was electric and obvious. However, they were just friends. She'd been repeating that sentiment to remind herself not to let the feeling linger too long. However, here she was two days later and she was still feeling the excitement. She sat down at her desk and turned on a CD featuring her favorite old-school R & B artist. As she bobbed her head to the music and polished her presentation for the staff meeting, she heard Jordan's voice in the hall. Within a matter of moments, he was standing in her office. He closed the door behind him and sat in one of the chairs in front of Chriselle's desk. He listened to the music for a few minutes and patted his foot to the rhythm as well. Neither said a word as the CD advanced to the next song. This song was special. It was their song back in the day. They both smiled when they heard it. Jordan stood up and walked around the desk to Chriselle. He extended his hand to her, and she hesitantly took it. He pulled her up, led her around the desk into a small open area in the office, pulled her close and began to serenade her as they swayed to the music. Chriselle allowed herself to relax into his arms.

"Chriselle, this is like heaven to me. I don't ever want to let you go," Jordan whispered.

Hearing Jordan's words reminded Chriselle this wasn't appropriate. She pulled herself away from his embrace.

"We can't go there, Jordan. It's over. It's been over and we need to keep our relationship purely professional."

"We already went there, Chriselle. I didn't force you to dance with me. I offered and you accepted."

"Okay, maybe I lost my mind for a moment. The fact is I am a married woman and some things are off-limits."

"I know all of that, but we both know what should've been. I respect the fact you're married to Drew, but, Chriselle, we were meant to be together. I don't know what that means for you and Drew, but know that's what I sincerely believe. I'd better get back to work." Jordan lightly kissed Chriselle's forehead.

Chriselle realized she needed to set clear boundaries and stick to them herself. Jordan wouldn't have any other choice but to follow suit. She had to admit that Jordan was definitely the fun-loving spontaneous man she remembered him to be, and she appreciated that about him. On the other hand, she was deeply in love with her husband. They had a family and therefore a history together, and one couldn't put a price tag on that. They were a team. They were solid. Chriselle would not allow Jordan or anyone else to interfere with that.

That evening Chriselle went home after work to find a brooding Drew. She noted a change in him some time ago but hadn't figured out what was going on with him.

"Something has been bothering you for a while. What is it? Talk to me, please," Chriselle begged as she stood in the kitchen.

Drew looked at her with something simmering in his eyes she couldn't quite identify but made her uncomfortable. She waited patiently to see if he would respond or if he would remain evasive. Thinking he wasn't going to answer her, Chriselle turned to go change her clothes and prepare for dinner.

"I came by your office the other day," Drew disclosed, as he moved to stand in front of his wife.

* * *

"Really?"

"Yes. Before I could get the car parked, I saw you walking toward your building. You were with your co-worker. What's his name? Jordan?"

"We were coming back from lunch, I think. Are you spying on me?"

"No, I've just been trying to surprise my wife. I know I've been working a lot of overtime so I thought we might steal a little time together during the day. This isn't the first time I've seen you out with him." Drew sat on a barstool.

"Well, I don't know what you're getting at, but..."

"I've just been feeling a little distance between us, especially since you went back to work. Am I just imagining things?"

"I haven't noticed any distance. I guess I'm not sure what you're feeling."

"Tell me about that guy Jordan."

"Is that what this is about? Jordan? Baby, he's someone from my past. We just happen to work in the same place. That's all. Why does that bother you?" Chriselle asked with outstretched arms.

"I've been thinking back to when I met you. I thought I

remembered something about a boyfriend you had. I didn't realize until recently that it was probably Jordan."

"None of that matters. I chose you and that relationship ended."

"Do you still think you made the right choice?"

"Honey, from the moment I saw you I knew you were the one God placed on this earth just for me. You were the right choice then and you are still the right choice now. My relationship with Jordan has been over for a long time now. It's well in the past."

Afterward, Chriselle thought about the conversation she just had with her husband. The truth was lately she wondered if she had truly dealt with her feelings for Jordan. When she married Drew, there was no doubt in her mind. He was the one. However, over time, things between them changed. Jordan was perfect for her right now. He was lively, active, outgoing and living life to the fullest. Drew was in a rut and she had unwittingly joined him there.

Chapter 8

"Oh, come on, Chriselle. Several of us have been taking classes to learn how to ballroom dance for a few weeks now. You should come with us." Chriselle's co-worker Sheila suggested.

"I don't know about that, Sheila. This is not a good time for me to be venturing out getting involved in new activities. My husband needs a little more attention right now." Chriselle said.

"It's only for an hour right after work. You'll probably beat him home, so he wouldn't even have to know about it."

"It does sound like fun and I have wanted to learn how to ballroom. I'll think about it, but no guarantees."

This conversation played over repeatedly in Chriselle's mind that evening as she waited for Drew. He was still working a lot of overtime, leaving Chriselle with little to do but watch TV, work on her crafts, and wait until he got home. It seemed so unfair since she could be at the dance classes doing something she believed she would enjoy. She asked Drew if he wanted to attend, but he declined, citing overtime and his clumsiness as his reasons. Drew couldn't be upset if she went. However, she wanted to insure there wouldn't be any more avoidable problems caused in their relationship.

Chriselle heard the garage door going up, indicating Drew's arrival at home. Chriselle had been trying to keep dinner warm for him since she didn't know exactly when he would get there. She stirred the mashed potatoes to insure they weren't dry and pulled the foil-wrapped pork chops from the oven as Drew entered the house. He removed his work shoes at the back door as he normally did and brought his lunch bag into the kitchen. He grunted what sounded like a hello to Chriselle and left the kitchen.

This was not his normal way of operating, so Chriselle decided to follow him to find out what happened to bring about this kind of attitude. But by the time she got to him, he was climbing into the shower. He typically conversed with her and ate dinner first, then took a shower. What was going on? In spite of her best efforts to reassure Drew, he still didn't seem happy. She didn't know what else she could do to bridge the gap in her marriage, but sitting around this house waiting for him to come in wasn't helping either one of them. Since he seemed to have made up his mind to be unhappy for some reason, she saw no need to be unhappy, too.

Chapter 9

Chriselle quickly wrote in her work journal. She was trying to
tie everything up so she could make it to the ballroom dance
class. It turned out her decision to attend was just the thing she
needed to feel better. She turned off the lights and locked her
office door. She was so excited about getting to class that she
didn't notice Jordan standing there waiting on her.

"You're in a good mood," Jordan said when Chriselle
unsuspectingly bumped into him in her rush.

"I am in a good mood," she responded, as the two of them
chuckled.

"Are you heading to class?" Jordan asked with hope in his eyes.

"I sure am. Are you going?" she asked him while fishing her car
keys out of her purse.

"Yes, I'm on my way there now. You want to head over with
me?"

"I need to get home right after the class, so I think I should
drive."

"There's no need in taking two cars, you know. I could drop you off at your car afterwards."

Chriselle gave Jordan a look reminding him he was over the line.

"What? I was just trying to be helpful. We can both ride in your car if it'll make you feel better. As high as gas prices are, I'll take all the help I can get," Jordan joked as the two shared a laugh again.

"All right, I guess it wouldn't hurt."

Jordan and Chriselle arrived at the restaurant banquet room just before the class was to begin. They wove their way through the diners on their way to their destination. Walking in, they found several co-workers who normally attended as well as a number of new faces. Altogether, the class had grown to more than fifty people. Chriselle surmised the organizers would soon have to find a larger venue for the event if it kept growing. Jordan gravitated toward the appetizer table while Chriselle found her way to Sheila. Shortly after arriving, the meet and greet portion ended and it was time to begin the lesson.

"Everyone needs to find a partner so we can get started," the instructor began.

As the group became couples, Chriselle couldn't find her regular partner. She noticed Jordan searching for his partner as well and hoped she wouldn't end up with him. They'd been successful at maintaining the boundaries she set to keep things completely professional and platonic. With her husband still wearing the title of "grumpiest husband in America," Chriselle just didn't need to do anything to add fuel to that fire in any way. Not only was she concerned about Drew's emotions; she was also becoming increasingly concerned about her own. Though she loved Drew, she began to notice the best times of her day were when she had innocent interaction with Jordan.

"I guess you and I are partners. Everyone else has a partner and I'm not dancing with another guy," Jordan whispered to Chriselle as it became apparent there were no other choices.

"I can dance with another guy."

"I was just joking. There isn't anyone left except you and me. What harm can it do?"

***

After the class was over, Jordan and Chriselle socialized with the other people that had gathered outside of the banquet room.

"Chriselle, are you in a rush to get home?" Jordan asked.

"I probably should. Drew hasn't been in the best of moods lately. Why do you ask?" Chriselle answered looking at her watch.

"I was thinking since we're here we might as well have a bite to eat. What do you say?"

Chriselle thought about Jordan's invitation. She was hungry and with Drew getting off late, he probably wouldn't be home for a while.

"Would you excuse me for a moment? I need to place a phone call."

"Sure. I'll be waiting right here."

Chriselle went to a semi-quiet corner and called Drew.

"Hi, Chriselle," Drew said when he answered the phone. "I'm still at work and can't talk long. Is everything okay?"

"Everything's fine, honey. I was just calling to see if you were still at work. I think I'm going to have a bite to eat while I'm out. Are you okay with that?"

"You've been hanging out quite a bit lately. What's going on?"

"Nothing really."

"Oh, okay."

"Well, I guess I'll see you at home then, Jordan."

"Whatever. Bye." Drew hung up with an obvious attitude

Chriselle didn't understand.

Chriselle searched for Jordan. Once she found him, she smiled and he held out his arm for her to loop hers through. The two walked to the host stand and requested seating for two.

While waiting for their food, Jordan and Chriselle held a very lively conversation. The laughter coming from their table wafted across the dining room, catching the attention of a couple sitting on the other side of the area.

***

"Wow, they're having a good time," the woman joked.

"Yes, they are. I think that's a good thing," the man sitting with her agreed.

"It is a good thing," she said thoughtfully. "For some reason, that laughter sounds really familiar. I don't want to be so obvious and turn around, but, for some reason, I think I need to see who that is."

The man looked over his wife's shoulder to see if he could identify who was laughing.

"Uh-oh," he said as his eyes landed on the source of the laughter. No wonder it sounded familiar.

"Who is it?"

"Um, I forgot I need to get home to work on a project for work. Can we get out of here?" The truth was he did have something he needed to finish for work. However, that was only part of it.

"Why do I feel like there's something you're trying to hide from me?"

"Uh, why would you say that?"

"I guess I'm just going to have to take a look for myself." She rotated her body in her chair so she could see the rest of the dining room. Allowing her eyes to roam the tables and booths in the area, her gaze landed on a woman throwing her head back in obvious enjoyment.

"Oh my goodness," Leslie exclaimed. "That's my mother! But who is that man?"

"I don't know, honey. I really think we should leave."

"No. I'm going over there."

"That's exactly what I was afraid of," Bryce lamented.

"I can't just pretend I didn't see this, you know."

"Please don't cause a scene in here. If we leave, you can take some time to figure out what, if anything, you should say to Chriselle."

"I'm not causing a scene. She's causing enough of a scene herself sitting over there with that man and laughing like he's telling Steve Harvey jokes. I'm sure he's not that funny. Why are they looking at each other like that? I'm going to find out what is going on." Leslie moved her chair back and stood.

"No. Listen, I have an idea. How about we walk past the table and if she sees us? We can pretend we just happened to be walking by. That'll open the door for you to find out who that man is," Bryce reasoned.

"Okay, we'll try it your way and see what happens."

Bryce took Leslie by the hand as they began to walk in the direction of her mother. Having her hand in his gave him the ability to pull her away if necessary. They approached the table and slowed as they faced Chriselle. Jordan and Chriselle never even looked up as Bryce and Leslie passed.

Chapter 10

"Momma, can I talk to you for a minute?" Leslie asked her mother during a family game night.

"Sure, baby. Just let me turn this oven off and we can talk." Chriselle turned off the oven, pulled the dishes of food out of it, and set them on the stove. She grabbed her daughter by the hand and walked over to a set of chairs out of earshot of most of the family. It seemed whatever Leslie wanted to talk about weighed heavily on her mind and Chriselle wanted her to be able to talk freely.

"So, what's on your mind?" Chriselle began.

"Bryce and I saw you the other night."

"Really? Where?"

"You weren't alone, Momma." Leslie sat back and crossed her legs.

"What are you getting at?" Chriselle asked.

"You were with a man."

"What did he look like?"

"Momma, how many men do you go to dinner with? Who was that?" Leslie's eyebrows rose.

"You must be talking about Jordan. He's an old friend and we work together. There was a whole group of people there taking a dance class."

"But I didn't see a whole group of people. You were at a table for two having what looked like a romantic dinner."

"You are making a big deal out of nothing, Leslie. It was just a meal. What's wrong with that?"

"Did Dad know you were just having a meal with a male friend?"

"No, not exactly." Chriselle shook her head.

"Then it is a big deal!"

"Why didn't you and Bryce come to the table?"

"Bryce suggested we walk by the table and we did. You were so into whatever this guy was saying, you didn't even notice us slow down."

"What? I don't believe it." Chriselle crossed her arms.
"It looked like you were on a date. Are you sure that's not the case?"

"It's not."

Leslie kneeled in front of Chriselle and held her hands.

"Momma, you need to end whatever it is because it doesn't look right. I notice Dad hasn't quite been himself lately, and here you are out there acting like a lovesick teenager. What's wrong with you?"

Chriselle began to examine her feelings for Jordan. She really didn't realize she'd begun to feel something a little more than friendly toward him. Working with him every day, going to lunch together, sometimes alone, and dance classes had definitely changed the way she saw him. Though she'd set boundaries and thought she was successful keeping Jordan at bay, she had to admit perhaps that somehow she'd lost the battle. She would sort those issues out later. The matter at hand was her daughter trying to tell her what she thought she should and shouldn't be doing.

"Did you just ask me what's wrong with me? What you need to remember is that you came from me and not the other way around. You've just been married a hot minute, so you wouldn't know how to advise me if there was a problem."

"Momma, you need to tell Dad or I —"

"Go right ahead. I will not have you threatening me. I don't know who you think you are, but don't you ever talk to me like that again. You might think you're grown, but I am real grown." Chriselle stomped away from the heated conversation with her daughter wondering why she was so defensive. Maybe Leslie was right, but her approach was disrespectful. Chriselle wasn't going to start that trend.

Chapter 11

Drew whistled as he exited his car and began the short trek to his destination. With flowers and a basket filled with lunch goodies, he entered the college administration building where his wife worked. Things between them had been tense lately and this surprise visit was an effort to alleviate it. Excitement prevented Drew from waiting for the elevator. Instead, he took the ivy-draped stairs to the second floor where Chriselle's office was located.

Drew talked the receptionist into allowing him to gain entry to his wife's office unannounced. He arrived at her office door and knocked lightly, causing the door to ease open. Realizing she wasn't there, he decided to set things up a little before she returned. He draped the round table in the room with a tablecloth and set the flowers in the center. While unpacking lunch, he heard Chriselle's voice coming closer. Hearing her distinctive laughter warmed his heart. It had been a while since he last heard it and wondered what was happening at work that drew this response. A man's voice followed by another bout of Chriselle's laughter answered his question. Undoubtedly, the man's voice belonged to Jordan. He had a feeling this relationship was the reason for the distance in their marriage. As he pondered the potential reality, the door opened and Jordan and Chriselle entered. Their light banter continued as Drew's presence went unnoticed.

Drew cleared his throat. Chriselle's mouth dropped open while Jordan was more poised.

"Hi, Drew. It is Drew, right?" Jordan asked as he smiled and extended his hand toward Drew.

"Yes. You're Jordan, right?" Drew responded without acknowledging Jordan's hand.

"Is everything okay?" Jordan wondered looking between Chriselle and Drew.

"Is it, Chriselle?" Drew asked.

"Um, yes. Everything is fine." Chriselle chuckled as she wrung her hands.

"Good. Drew, you have a wonderful wife."

* * *

"Oh yeah? Tell me. How do you know how wonderful my wife is?" Drew inquired aloud, sauntering toward Jordan.

"Jordan, would you mind leaving Drew and me to talk for a few minutes?"

"Are you sure? I'm not sure I'm too comfortable leaving you when I sense there's a problem."

"Isn't that something? You're going to protect my wife from me?" Drew questioned.

"Jordan, I'm fine. Just go, please," Chriselle begged as she pushed Jordan toward the door.

"Yes! Go, Jordan," Drew shouted.

Jordan hesitated as he left the room. The grin on his face ignited fresh anger in Drew making him clench his fists, as Chriselle stood between the men.

A crooked grin graced Jordan's face as he was pushed from the room. "It's nice to see you again, Drew. I'll see you later, Chriselle," Jordan commented as he left.

"Are you over him?" Drew asked his wife.

"Drew, I keep telling you there's nothing going on."

Drew narrowed his eyes. "You didn't answer the question. Are you still in love with Jordan?"

"In love? Who said I was ever in love?"

"This man was basically your fiancé. You had to have significant feelings for him."

"He's a dear friend; that's all."

Drew shook his head. "I don't buy it, Chriselle. You've been running around the house unhappy. I haven't heard you laugh or seen a smile in weeks. You called me by his name the other day. Then I come in here and you're having a laughing good time with him. Now, tell me again about you and Jordan just being friends."

"Wait, I called you by his name? That did not happen. I don't know what your problem is. There is nothing wrong with me having lunch or whatever with Jordan. It's the same as if he were a female friend."

"Yeah, but he's not just a female friend, now, is he?" Drew took the basket and exited the office, leaving Chriselle to ponder what had just happened.

Chapter 12

Drew lifted Chriselle's luggage out of the trunk of the car at baggage check outside the airport terminal. He rolled the bags to the counter and checked them for his wife.

"Thanks for bringing me to the airport, honey."

"Don't thank me. I'm not comfortable with you going to this conference."

"I know you're uncomfortable but there's really no reason for you to feel that way."

Chriselle and Drew stood at the curbside repeating the same conversation they'd had numerous times since Chriselle was assigned to attend the conference for the department.

Jordan walked up with his luggage trailing behind him and a huge smile on his face. "Good morning, you two."

"Good morning," Chriselle responded.

"Whatever," Drew mumbled.

"I'll wait for you inside, Chriselle," Jordan said.

"Yeah, do that, Jordan," Drew said.

"Calm down. Everything's going to be okay." Chriselle placed her hand on her husband's chest.

"All right. I just want to remind you. I don't like this. Make sure you keep him in his place."

"I'll see you in a few days, honey."

Chriselle and Drew shared a kiss, and she disappeared into the airline terminal. As Drew drove away, he looked into the airport and noticed Jordan and Chriselle interacting as though they were newlyweds going on a honeymoon.

***

"The sessions today were amazing. I learned a lot," Chriselle said as she walked alongside Jordan toward their hotel rooms.

"I see how I can utilize some of what we learned right away."

"Don't forget we have to put together a report for the department so we can share the information."

"Why don't we work on the report together? I'm sure we each learned some things the other didn't," Jordan suggested.

"That might be a good idea."

"Your room or mine?" Jordan said, leaning on the wall with folded arms, waiting for Chriselle's response.

"Neither. I'm going to freshen up, and I'll meet you in the lobby in an hour. Bye, Jordan."

"We can order room service."

"Bye, Jordan," Chriselle said as she entered her hotel room.

An hour later, Chriselle exited the elevator and entered the lobby with the supplies needed to put together the conference report required by the college. She looked around the lobby. Not seeing Jordan, she assumed he hadn't arrived yet. She looked for an available table and found none. She saw a couple of open tables in the bar area and decided to head there.

"Hey, I was looking for you," Jordan said, walking up to her.

"I was just looking for somewhere we can sit."

"I don't think the bar will be quiet enough. The lobby is no better. I told you, we should do this upstairs," Jordan said, peeking into the bar area.

"No. If my husband found out, that wouldn't be good. Drew had enough of a problem with me coming on this trip. I'm not going to give him any more reason to be upset."

"We're just working. That's all."

"That's out of the question."

"Why don't we make it a working dinner? The concierge told

me about a nice restaurant about a block down. After we get the report done, we can head over to the jazz club across the street to close out our time here at the conference."

Chriselle nodded in agreement. "I guess I could stand to have a bite to eat. I'm not so sure about going to the jazz club. I'll probably be ready to go back to the hotel, relax, and wait for Drew's call."

"I'll make sure you're back to the hotel in time to take Drew's call and you can relax on the plane. What do you say?"

"We'll see how I feel after dinner."

***

Chriselle and Jordan sat at a table in the back of the jazz club as the band began to play. After several songs, Chriselle looked at her watch and realized she had lost track of time. Panicking, she pulled her cell phone from her purse and noticed a number of missed phone calls, all from Drew. As she prepared to call him, the phone rang once again and she answered.

"Hi Drew."

"I've been trying to call you! Is everything okay?

"Yes, everything is okay. I'm sorry I missed your calls."

"As long as you're okay, that's all that matters." At that

moment, the band launched into their next selection.

"Where are you? I hear music."

"We decided to go to a jazz club after dinner since it's our last night here."

"We?"

"Before you get the wrong idea, Jordan and I…"

"With all the people who went to the conference from the college, you and Jordan decided to go listen to some jazz. After dinner. Alone."

"Is there a problem?" Chriselle said as she motioned to Jordan that she was excusing herself from the table.

"Hurry back," Jordan said as she left.

"Is that Jordan I hear? I have had enough of him," Drew growled.

"Don't be upset. It really is innocent."

"I know you keep saying there's nothing to be concerned about, but he is anything but innocent and it's becoming a big issue. I need you to listen to me. I am not going to continue putting up with you hanging out with Jordan any longer regardless of how you describe your relationship. You need to fix this, Chriselle. I don't care how you do it—fix it."

• • •

"But, Drew …"

"Good night, Chriselle. I don't want to talk about this over the phone and definitely not in front of him. This needs to be a private conversation between us. I'll see you when you get home. I'll be at the airport when your plane lands. Look for me where I dropped you off."

"Okay. I love you."

"I love you, too, Chriselle."

Chapter 13

Chriselle walked into the vending area of the department's break room and noticed Jordan sitting there. His back was to her as he gazed out of the wall of windows overlooking the wooded grounds surrounding the campus. This allowed her a few moments to decide whether to have the conversation with him that should have taken place years before. The change in her husband's attitude and her daughter's revelation drove Chriselle to face the facts. Jordan wasn't over her and she wasn't sure what she felt about him. She purchased a couple of items from the machine and forced herself to walk over to where Jordan sat before she lost her nerve.

"You seem deep in thought," Chriselle said as she approached Jordan's table.

"I am. Have a seat," Jordan replied.

"Are you sure you don't want to be alone with your thoughts?'

"It's okay. Come on and sit," Jordan said as he pulled out a chair for Chriselle.

"How has your day been so far?"

"It's been pretty good, but it just got better."

"Why would that be?"

"Because you just showed up." The two sat in silence watching two deer frolic in the trees as they processed Jordan's comment.

"We need to talk," Chriselle suggested.

"About?"

"About us."

"You've been telling me there is no us. So what's there to say?"

"I want to clear the air, and you know what I'm talking about."

"I'm listening." Jordan sat back with crossed arms.

"I know we had an agreement that we'd wait on each other when we went away to college."

"I thought we did, but apparently I was wrong."

"No, you're right. We did agree we would get married after we got out of college," Chriselle acknowledged with a nod.

"But somehow you married someone else before we even had a chance."

"Jordan, we were just too young to make that kind of commitment," Chriselle explained

"That's not how I felt. I lived my life according to that promise."

"You didn't date anyone?"

"Yes, I went out on dates. But I always knew things couldn't go any further because we were supposed to be in a committed relationship," Jordan explained.

"We weren't in the same state. We didn't even see each other very often. You had to know our relationship wasn't solid." Chriselle avoided Jordan's gaze.

"Again, I didn't get into another relationship because I thought I was already in one. Obviously, you didn't see it that way."

"Honestly, I thought the same as you. We were committed. As time went on, that changed. I met new people and experienced different things that changed me as a person. After a while, I guess I didn't see you as my boyfriend anymore."

"That hurts." Jordan's shoulders drooped.

"I can't believe it still hurts all these years later."

"You obviously didn't know how much in love with you I was and still am."

Jordan and Chriselle turned their attention back to the playing deer.

"I'm sorry, Jordan. Nothing can come of us. I'm married."

"Chriselle, I know you're married, but I also know you're not happy. That relationship doesn't meet your needs at this point in your life. I know you well enough to know that much."

"You're wrong," Chriselle lied. "Everything is good between Drew and me."

"Well, what about all the time we spend together at dance classes, lunch, and even that day at the gathering? Not to mention the time we were away at the conference. You were enjoying all of that with me. You can't tell me that didn't mean anything to you."

Chriselle took a few moments to ponder her response. She knew Jordan was right. There was something still brewing between them no matter how hard she fought it.

"Okay, I can't deny that. But that just means there are some residual feelings."

Jordan turned his chair toward Chriselle and scooted forward a little. He leaned in toward her.

"It means we are soul mates. It means you need to give us a chance to see where this thing can go. You cheated us out of it before. I think you owe it to us to at least give it a shot."

"Am I supposed to just go tell Drew I'm leaving and pack up my stuff? Come on, Jordan. You can't be serious."

"Listen, I'm considering taking a job out of state. You should come with me. You've lived the first part of your adult life for him and the kids. Now, it's time for you to do something for yourself. I know you're bored with your life and I'm confident I can give you what you need. If you're honest with yourself—I already started."

Chapter 14

Chriselle had a lot on her mind as she drove home from work that day. She knew she needed to have a conversation of some sort with Drew. Some things needed saying and they had waited long enough. No matter what she decided to do, someone was going to be hurt. She didn't realize how deeply Jordan felt for her. Perhaps she convinced herself it was just infatuation between two teenagers so she wouldn't have to acknowledge how intense it really was. Choosing to ignore the promise they made to each other was much easier that way.

However, Drew and Chriselle had history together. Chriselle had raised children with Drew, struggled through many challenges with him, seen him sick, knew what made him tick and tock, fought and loved. That was true of any long-term relationship. No matter what they encountered, their love only grew and matured. Drew was more than just her husband. He was her rock, her lover, her closest friend and confidante. He was stable, caring, dependable and supportive. Chriselle never once had to worry about whether she would have what she needed or wanted. Drew's goal in life was to insure Chriselle's happiness. Nothing had ever happened between them that caused Chriselle to question whether they would be together forever—until now.

Jordan filled a void she'd been missing in her life. That place where she could just be and enjoy the moment. Everything with him was easy, fulfilling, and fun. Jordan fed parts of her that Drew's lack of attention starved. Though she'd known Jordan longer than she'd known Drew, they hadn't faced anything together. All they'd ever had were good times. She didn't even recall them having a major disagreement. That explained why everything seemed so enjoyable with Jordan. Life hadn't happened to them. There had been no testing. However, why should that keep her from seeing what a new relationship with Jordan might bring? She enjoyed who she was when she was with him. Wasn't it time she indulged herself?

The little angel on her shoulder reminded her of the vows she'd made to Drew. She was keenly aware of that. Maybe she should give them a chance to become like her and Jordan now that the children were gone and they could focus on each other. Drew's ideas of what that life would look like were different from hers, but that didn't mean they were etched in stone.

By the time she pulled into the driveway, she knew what she needed to communicate to Drew. She pulled her body out of the car and moved toward the door. As she put the key in the door, it opened. Drew was standing there with a huge smile on his face. Chriselle didn't know what put it there, but she hadn't seen it in what felt like a long time. She smiled, too.

"Drew, can you come in the kitchen? I want to talk to you about something." Chriselle sighed as she entered their home and moved toward the kitchen island with her husband following.

"What's going on?"

"I hope you'll understand what I'm about to say."

"Sounds serious."

"It is."

Sitting on a barstool at the island, Drew waited as Chriselle considered what she would say once again. No matter what she said, Drew wasn't going to be happy. Jordan would only be happy if he got his way. The point of this conversation, though, was to free Chriselle.

"I haven't been completely honest about my relationship with Jordan," Chriselle said as she sat next to Drew.

* * *

"I know."

"How did you know?" Chriselle asked.

Drew's eyebrows rose. "I've been married to you for more years than I wasn't. You don't think I notice when things are different?"

"I guess I didn't realize it was so obvious." Chriselle looked away as she remembered Leslie informing her of how things appeared.

"You said you need to talk. I'm listening." Drew folded his arms.

"Let me start at the beginning. Jordan and I were engaged in a way. We promised to get married after we graduated from college."

"So, let me get this straight, you were engaged to him when we got married?"

"I guess you could say that. If we'd had our way, we would've gotten married the day after high school graduation. Our parents talked us into waiting until we finished college before we made that commitment. I met and married you before Jordan and I had a chance to see where our relationship would go." Chriselle waved her hands to emphasize her words.

"Do you regret that?" Drew winced awaiting her response.

Chriselle swiveled her chair to face Drew as she prepared to speak. "I do, but only from the standpoint that Jordan and I didn't have proper closure on our relationship. He came home thinking we would be together only to find out that wasn't true. He wasn't prepared for that and it has affected him over the years."

"Forgive me for saying this, but I really don't care how Jordan feels. He's a grown man and none of my concern."

"I understand. But I felt extremely guilty once I found out how my decision hurt him."

Drew stood and took a few steps away before turning to Chriselle. "Well, what about now?" Once again, Drew winced.

"I'm getting to that. When I ran into Jordan at work, he began to pursue me. He wanted the chance to have the relationship we'd planned when we were younger. I have to admit, I enjoy the attention. I enjoy the time Jordan and I spend together. We have fun where you and I have grown a little, well, stale."

"Wow! That stings."

"You were talking about riding off into the sunset on a pontoon boat and fishing from the shore. That wasn't my idea of how I wanted to live the rest of my life." Chriselle released the breath she had apparently been holding in.

"What does a pontoon boat have to do with all of this?"

"It feels like you want to slow life down to a creep while I want to rev things up a bit."

"Why do you think I don't want to try new things?"

"You never want to do the things I want to do. I enjoy doing some of those things with my co-workers."

"Including Jordan."

"Yes, including Jordan."

"I see. It sounds like your relationship with him went a little too far. Am I right?"

"I've been true to our marriage from the beginning."

Drew slammed his hands on the counter. "No, you haven't. Let's be clear here. You're having an emotional affair with your high school sweetheart. That is not being true to us."

"Honestly, Drew, I got caught up. I felt I owed it to myself to determine whether I wanted to keep that door open or close it completely. Ideally, that would have happened before I got into a relationship with you. It didn't." Chriselle stood, moving to stand face-to-face with her husband.

"You're infatuated with this guy. It can't be love. Right?" Drew paused a beat.

"All I can say is, when I'm with Jordan, I feel alive. It's exciting. Do I believe I'm in love with Jordan? No, we don't share the type of love you and I do. But I need to get out there and experience life in a different way. Do you understand?"

"This is too much, Chriselle." Drew placed his hands on his waist and began to pace.

Chriselle wondered what he was thinking, though she was sure it wasn't positive. Silence became the third person in the room.

"Drew?" Tears flowed from Chriselle's eyes.

"I'm thinking."

The silence continued.

Finally, he said, "Is this about your feelings for Jordan or us being stale?"

"Maybe a little of both."

"You know, the more I think about it, I don't buy it, Chriselle. You can't convince me this isn't about your feelings for Jordan. I haven't changed and you haven't complained until now. So, don't blame me for your desire to do what you want to do."

"That's not true."

"Let me tell you something else. I'm done sitting around wondering what's going on with you. You need to decide what you want to do and let's get on with it. You aren't the only one that wants to enjoy their life." Drew said as he turned to leave the room.

"I know exactly what I want," Chriselle said.

Drew turned toward his wife, waiting for her to reveal something that could change the course for them as a couple for the rest of their lives.

Chapter 15

The salsa music started and the couple began to move with the rhythm in the cruise ship's dance club. Chriselle's flippy skirt performed its own dance as she kicked, dipped, spun and twirled at the direction of her partner. As sweat popped up on each of their faces, the man limited their movement so their bodies could recover. When the song ended, Chriselle attempted to lead her man off the dance floor.

"Where are you going, woman? I'm just getting warmed up," he teased.

"I'm a little tired," Chriselle replied.

"Un unh. That's not acceptable. You wanted to dance, so we're going to dance."

They returned to the dance floor as a slower song began to play, giving Chriselle a short reprieve.

"I didn't know you could dance so well, Drew."

"Just because dancing is your thing doesn't mean I can't do a little something-something."

"I see that," Chriselle said as Drew dipped her. "I can't wait to go zip lining at the next port."

"Wait a minute. We agreed we're doing something I want to do tomorrow," Drew reminded his wife.

"You're right. I forgot," Chriselle said as she and drew drifted across the dance floor.

"We can do zip lining if there's time."

"You know what? I'm glad we were able to work this out."

"Me, too. I know I shouldn't bring him up, but, what happened to Jordan?" Drew wondered.

"Since I left the college, I don't have occasion to see him anymore. I heard he took a job out of state," Chriselle responded.

"Good, then we won't be running into him anywhere. Now, let's change the subject. Let's go see a show. I heard the music revue on this ship is amazing. How does that sound?"

"I would love to, honey."

Chriselle and Drew left the dance floor hand-in-hand headed toward the theater. Chriselle felt content and at peace with her decision to remain in her marriage. While spending time with Jordan was exciting and new, she realized being in the presence of the newly retired Drew was just as invigorating. Though their marriage was mature, they still managed to learn a new skill...compromise. When Drew wanted to go out on the pontoon boat, Chriselle obliged and actually learned to enjoy those peaceful moments. When she wanted to do something like off-roading, Drew compromised and went with her. Chriselle realized she already had the perfect man for her right at home, and they would remain together until death parted them.

Questions for Reflection

Do you think Jordan's intentions were honorable?

Was Jordan motivated by his love for Chriselle or winning?

Is Chriselle in love with two men? Is that possible?

Does Chriselle owe it to herself to explore the relationship possibilities with Jordan or remain with Drew and potentially be unhappy?

Did Chriselle ever fully get over Jordan?

Do you think Chriselle outgrew Drew?

Does Drew take Chriselle for granted? Does Chriselle take Drew for granted?

What role does Drew's lack of interests outside of his job play in the staleness of their marriage?

Did Chriselle and Jordan have an emotional affair?

Is there a problem with having friends of the opposite sex when one is married? Is it okay to have lunch, dinner or meet for other events with that person?

Chriselle mentioned she enjoyed the attention Jordan gave her. What do you think that says about Chriselle?

Do you think a relationship between Chriselle and Jordan could work? Why or why not?

Were the feelings Chriselle and Jordan experienced in *Twice Bitten* based on what they remembered about each other as teens?

Would you stay in an unhappy relationship simply out of loyalty?

The typical wedding vows include a promise to stay married until death. Do you feel this only applies to physical death?

Do you think one who is truly in love can fall out of love at some point?

If you were Chriselle, how would you respond to this dilemma? What would you do?

Darliss Batchelor

Hell

is a

Skyscraper

Chapter 1

"Evelyn, I'm going over to Neely's to fix something at her place."

"This late? Why can't you do it tomorrow?"

"She called me yesterday and I just didn't make it over there. It sounded important."

"All right then. Get on back as soon as possible."

Walking to his wife and giving her a peck on the lips, he responded, "I'll be right back." Leaving their half of the duplex, Julius stopped, remembering something else he needed to address with Evelyn. "I might as well pay the rent while I'm there. Do you have it?"

Evelyn slowly pushed herself out of her chair. She went to their bedroom to get her purse and retrieve the money for the rent.

Why her parents left this duplex to her sister, Neely, she didn't understand. For some reason, they thought Neely was a better choice to care for the family's home when they passed away.

When Evelyn questioned their wishes, her mother told her it was her father's decision, while her father claimed it was her mother's choice.

Evelyn's feelings were hurt when she found out Neely would take over the family home where they all grew up. It didn't matter now whose decision it was, Evelyn and her family needed a place to live and this was it. At least Neely allowed them to move in after their eviction from their previous rented home.

However, Neely could be so unreasonable about their rent being on time and the exact amount. If they were a penny short or a day late, she would lose her head and threaten to put her, Julius, and her children out on the street. Whether Neely would really follow through with her threat Evelyn wasn't sure, but she was certainly convincing if she was bluffing. With her husband barely working and her disability check being so small, she had to cut corners where necessary to make ends meet while satisfying Neely's demands.

Like tonight, Neely always had a chore or something for Julius to do. If it wasn't Julius, it was their son Demetri. Evelyn often wondered why Neely didn't get one of her many boyfriends to make repairs for her. Certainly, one of them was handy. Evelyn concluded Neely just liked having her brother-in-law and nephew jump whenever she called.

Evelyn suspected her sister was jealous of the fact that she was married and Neely had never been. Being the older sister and the more outgoing of the two, most would have thought Neely would be married first. However, Neely never had the privilege of experiencing even one proposal though she dated half the male population in their small town.

Evelyn hobbled back to the living room and gave the money to Julius so he could take it to Neely. She hoped he remembered to get a receipt so they would have proof of the cash payment. Evelyn never knew when Neely was going to try to get one over on them. A person couldn't put very much past Neely.

With Julius gone, Evelyn went in search of her nine-year-old son, Demetri. Vanessa, Demetri's thirteen-year-old sister, had long outgrown the bedtime ritual Evelyn was seeking her son for. She walked into her daughter's room thinking she might find him there, but Vanessa was its only inhabitant. She walked past the bathroom thinking she might find him in her bedroom. Suddenly, she heard his voice in the bathroom, stopping her in her tracks. She wondered to whom he was talking. Placing her ear close to the door, she realized he was talking to God. Feeling as though she shouldn't infringe on his privacy, she started to walk away. However, when she heard him crying, she returned to knock on the door.

"Demetri, are you in there?"

Demetri sniffled and responded, "Yes." It was obvious he tried to remove the tears from his voice, but his mother wasn't fooled. She'd already heard him crying.

"When you're done, come out to the living room. I have a special story for you tonight."

"I'll be there in a few minutes, Momma."

Evelyn had noticed her son's sadness on several occasions before now. She'd asked him if everything was okay and he'd assured her everything was fine. She didn't believe him because she knew him better than he knew himself. But with no input from him, it was difficult to help if she didn't know what the problem was. She'd been praying about this particular situation from the moment she first noticed the change in his demeanor.

Evelyn felt led to talk to her son even more about God's love in situations that may not be the best. She was going to talk to him about Joseph tonight because that was what she believed God was directing her to do. She didn't understand it all, but she knew well enough to be obedient to what she believed was God's direction regardless.

Eventually Demetri showed up for their nightly ritual, reading bible stories, praying, or whatever the two decided to do during "their time." His eyes were a bit puffy still and his nose a little red, but he did his best to hide his feelings. He crawled up next to his mother and snuggled up. She hugged him back and the two sat in silence for a brief period. There was silent communication between them. His mother confirmed her love for him and he let her know he believed her.

"Demetri, is there anything special you want to talk about tonight?"

Demetri looked as though he thought about saying something but quickly changed his mind and shook his head. Evelyn was disappointed because she knew something was going on and wanted desperately to help her son with whatever it was. She did take comfort in knowing he went to God with his concerns. Ultimately, it would take God to fix it regardless of who knew anyway, but it was natural for a mother to want to get involved as well.

"Do you remember when we talked about Joseph before?"

"Did he have that coat with all those colors?"

"That's him. God had a very special assignment for him. He spoke to Joseph through dreams."

"His dreams got him into trouble, didn't they?"

"Well, his brothers were angry because of a dream he had."

"Then they made him a slave."

"Yes, they did. He had many bad things happen to him after that. But, God still spoke to him through his dreams and visions. In the end, Joseph ended up right where God wanted him to be. You have a special assignment from God, too. We don't know exactly what it is yet, but I know it's there. Do you know what that assignment is called?"

"It's my calling."

"Yes, baby, it's your calling. I see you have been paying attention to me, haven't you?"

"Yes, Momma, I always listen to you. I'm not like Vanessa."

"I know, Demetri. I want you to remember that when things get hard and you go through difficult situations, it's part of the preparation for your calling. Don't be afraid. God is always with you. Momma and Daddy may not be there, but He will be. In the end, no matter what you go through, you'll get to the place where God wants you."

"What kind of difficult situations?"

"I don't know, but I think you're going through one now."

Demetri looked away from his mother once again at the mention of his problem. Again, he looked as though he debated telling his mother the nature of the issue.

"I am, Momma. But you taught me to talk to God about it and that's what I've been doing. Now I understand it might be because of my calling."

"That's right, baby. It's because of your calling."

. . .

Chapter 2

Dear Demetri's Diary,

I knew Momma was sick, but I didn't know just how sick she was. Looking back at it as a grown man today, Momma was preparing me for her home going. She died a short time after this conversation. I loved those moments when she would cuddle me and teach me from the word of God. I don't know how she knew, but Momma found out somehow that I was in some kind of trouble. What I learned from this is that God will take care of me and He'll be right there for me no matter how hard things got. With what was happening in my life at the time, this was valuable information. I knew I had to lean on God because I soon learned I had no one else to turn to.

Chapter 3

"We've got to figure out how things are going to work now that your mother's gone," Julius said as Vanessa and Demetri sat sadly at the kitchen table.

"I just can't believe Momma's gone. It was so quick. I don't know what I'm going to do without my mother!" Vanessa cried.

"I'll tell you what we're going to do. We're going to keep living. It's what your mother would've wanted," Julius said, trying to encourage his children.

"I want Momma back," Demetri yelled with tears streaming from his eyes.

Neely came in the house and sat down at the table with the other family members. Vanessa's face lit up like a light bulb while Demetri sighed and let his head fall to the table. Neely wore what appeared to be one of her Sunday best ensembles complete with a feathered hat, rhinestone jewelry, and high-heeled sling-back pumps all in a deep shade of pink. Her face was flawlessly made-up, including her fuchsia pink lips.

"I went down to the funeral home and paid for the services so we can bury Evelyn." Neely spoke as she looked around at the bereaved family with a questioning look. "I don't know why y'all are looking so sad. Evelyn is in a better place. She doesn't have to worry about anything now."

"She can't be in a better place because we're not there with her!" Demetri yelled, as if speaking louder would change the reality of the situation.

"Look here, boy. Your momma is dead so there's no reason for you to be acting like that with me. You know what I'll do for you so you just need to get yourself together," Neely warned with a pointed finger and the other hand on her hip. "What's going on anyway, Julius? It looks like there was a meeting going on I should be a part of."

"Auntie Neely, we're talking about how different things are going to be without Momma," Vanessa said.

"What did you tell them, Julius?"

"I haven't said anything yet. We were just talking."

"It's clear to me what needs to happen. Vanessa is going to have to step up and be the woman of the house. She'll have to cook the meals, clean the house, and do the laundry."

• • •

"I don't know how to do any of that! Momma never got around to teaching me. She said I was too young to be trying to do all of that because she wanted me to be a teenager as long as possible." Vanessa pleaded with her aunt.

"You don't have a choice. I'll teach you as much as I can, but I don't cook much myself being single and all. You're going to have to learn that skill on your own and you need to do it well because I come over here to eat, too. Demetri, you're going to have to start doing some stuff around the house too because your mother babied you too much. Your daddy is going to have to find another job or two to pay me my rent since your mother took her disability check right along with her. You're going to have to take out the trash at least. I got some things at my apartment for you to do so don't think you're off the hook because you're not."

Chapter 4

Dear Demetri's Diary,

I remember Auntie Neely telling me that I was going to have to pick up some of the slack left by my father's need to work more. The last thing I needed to deal with at that point was my Auntie Neely. She never seemed to like anyone except maybe Vanessa and here she was telling her she had to grow up before her time and take care of the family the way Momma did. Vanessa never could replace Momma, no more than I could take Daddy's place. It was extremely stressful trying to satisfy unreasonable Auntie Neely and grieving, too. I missed my mother so much and I still do. There's not a day that goes by that I don't think about her. Things were bad then, but they were about to get worse. After Momma died, I experienced the full depth of hell that was to come.

Chapter 5

Julius, Neely, Vanessa, and Demetri attended church for the first time since Evelyn died. The family took a month off to grieve and readjust to life without such an integral part of their lives. Early in the morning, Auntie Neely entered and woke everyone up. She ordered everyone to be dressed in thirty minutes so Vanessa only had a few minutes to fix a small breakfast for the family. She was still working on trying to be the woman of the house. It was extremely difficult for her with school and Auntie Neely breathing down her neck, but she was trying. In twenty-nine minutes, everyone was dressed, fed, and ready to head to church.

The four walked into the sanctuary and right down the center aisle, first Neely, then Julius, with Vanessa and Demetri lumbering behind. The pastor acknowledged their presence before bringing the morning message.

"I'm so glad to see y'all this morning. I know you had it rough after Evelyn went on to be with the Lord. But God saw fit to leave you here in the land of the living. We know you loved her, but God loved her most. If there's anything we can do for you, just let us know and we'll do it for you if we can. Isn't that right, church?"

"Sho' nuff, Pastor! They're a part of us!" the church replied.

"We're still praying for you, but if you need someone to cook a meal or clean house, call us. Brother Julius, if you find yourself in need of someone to help with Vanessa or Demetri, please let us know. If we can't help, we'll find someone who can. God bless you."

After service, Demetri and Vanessa were ready to go home. However, Auntie Neely seemed to enjoy greeting everyone and telling them about how much of a mess Evelyn's family was and how she had to fix everything. Hearing her talk about their mother in such an uncomplimentary way was both irritating and inconsiderate.

"Hello, Demetri and Vanessa. How are you two doing?" Sister Richardson walked up and greeted her Sunday school student and his big sister.

"Hi, Sister Richardson. We're okay," Vanessa replied with a pasted on grin.

"That's wonderful, Vanessa. Demetri, how are you?"

Demetri looked up at his teacher. She taught him so many of the same things his mother did. He loved Sister Richardson for that.

"I'm good."

"I miss you in Sunday school. I hope you're coming back soon. We're getting ready to talk about the story of Joseph."

Chapter 6

Dear Demetri's Diary,

Sister Richardson was like a cool breeze and a tall glass of iced tea on the hottest summer day. She was my last link to God's love and understanding. She showed that love to me and her concern for me was an invaluable blessing, as I would soon learn.

When Sister Richardson told me my Sunday school class was going to be discussing Joseph, I knew God was trying to tell me something. I was ready to see what I needed to get out of this young man's life. I remember Momma telling me about Joseph. He was his father's favorite, it seemed, based on him giving Joseph the coat of many colors. God allowed him to dream and to discern the meaning of other people's dreams. The thing that stuck out to me the most was how he went through all of those troubles. As a man looking back over my life, I've certainly lived through my fair share of difficulties.

Chapter 7

Demetri got dressed, did his chores and stationed himself at the kitchen table to do his homework so he could watch television for a while. It was the weekend so there was a lot on television he wanted to see. Daddy came home from work to a request from Auntie Neely for him to come by her place. Daddy obviously didn't want to go, but it was just as obvious he knew he had to.

"Neely, how about I send Demetri over there? He can take care of that for you. I worked two shifts today and I'm tired."

Demetri looked up at his father with disbelief. He didn't want to be the sacrificial lamb. He considered complaining of a stomachache or something to avoid going to Auntie Neely's place. Demetri also considered running away from home on occasion for the same reason. In fact, he would rather do all of his chores as well as Vanessa's if his sister could go in his place. Vanessa was crazy about Auntie Neely so it wouldn't be a problem for her.

Demetri begged his father not to make him go. Didn't he know what Auntie Neely was like? No matter what kind of deal he tried to cut with his father in lieu of going next door his father wouldn't relent.

"Boy, you are just going to have to take this. We need this place to stay and with your momma gone, it's hard to pay the rent every month. The least you could do is take care of what your Auntie Neely wants sometimes."

"But, Dad..."

"I'm done talking about it. Now finish your homework and get over there in about a half hour."

A little over an hour later, Demetri was still sitting at the table taking more time than necessary to finish his homework. Julius walked into the kitchen and noticed Demetri still sitting there. When Julius looked at the clock on the wall, he turned to his son and said, "Demetri, I thought I told you to go over to help Neely."

"You did," Demetri responded.

"Well, why are you still sitting there?"

"I'm finishing my homework and I didn't notice how much time went by. Once I finish this assignment, I'll go."

"No, you're going to have to finish that homework after you get back."

"But, Dad, you and Momma always told me to get my school work done before I do anything else. This is really important."

"Close the book and put your supplies away. Do what I told you."

"But can't it wait until tomorrow?"

Julius lost his temper and grabbed the boy from his chair at the table. Demetri fought Julius as he dragged him toward the door. The boy tried to gain traction with his feet in order to stop the progress. He placed his hands on the doorposts to resist his father pulling him through it. When that didn't work, he put his feet there, too, all to no avail. Julius pushed Demetri out of their side of the duplex onto the porch and then through Neely's door. All the while, Demetri begged his father not to do this to him. Focusing on getting Demetri next door, Julius didn't hear his son's pleas.

Once Demetri was inside, his father pointed his finger at him as if giving a silent warning and closed the door. Demetri sniffled and silently prayed to the God his mother and Sister Richardson taught him about to rescue him. He didn't know what to expect except something bad. Nothing good ever came out of being alone with Auntie Neely. Standing in the silence, Demetri heard his stomach rumble. Since he didn't hear or see Auntie Neely, he decided to go into the kitchen to look for something to eat. In the pantry, he found a box of his favorite chocolate cereal and in the refrigerator; he found a gallon of milk. Demetri decided this would be his snack.

The bowls were up high in the cabinet since they didn't get much use. He pulled up a chair near the cabinet and stood on it to get a bowl. Pouring the milk and cereal into the bowl, Demetri thought perhaps his aunt had run out or something, providing him a reprieve. Maybe God heard his prayer and saved him from whatever Auntie Neely planned. He decided to eat the cereal and if Auntie Neely wasn't here by then he would leave. He certainly didn't want to make his father any angrier than he was. He ate the cereal and just as he was about to leave, a sudden streak of red came towards him. Neely wore a long silk kimono-style robe with solid red trim and jewel-toned flowers covering it. She turned the chair Demetri sat in over backwards, sending him to the floor, and victimized her nephew in a new and unexpected way.

Once Aunt Neely finished with him, he ran home crying. He ran through the house looking for Vanessa to show her what happened. When he found her, she saw how distraught he was and came to his aid.

"Slow down and breathe. Tell me what's wrong."

He removed his hands from his face and she saw that his eyebrows were gone. Auntie Neely took clippers to them for some reason and erased them from his face.

"What happened to you?"

"Auntie Neely did this to me. I don't know why she hates me so much."

"I don't know why you're lying on her. Why would she do that to you?"

"Because she hates me! Didn't you hear me the first time?"

"Stop lying. Just admit you were playing with Dad's clippers or something and messed up your face."

"That's not what happened," he told her.

It was clear Vanessa didn't believe him and that was because Auntie Neely didn't treat her the way she treated him. Though that was the case, Demetri still thought Vanessa of all people would listen and believe him. Apparently, he thought wrong because she leapt up from her bed and ran into Dad's room to tell him Demetri was lying on Auntie Neely.

* * *

When she told him, he looked at his son's face so obviously missing eyebrows and shook his head. Keeping his head lowered, he told his children to leave the room then began staring into space. Vanessa and Demetri left the room dumbfounded and went to their respective spaces. There was no help coming from him one way or the other.

Chapter 8

Dear Demetri's Diary,

It was at that moment I began to lose hope. Auntie Neely had been abusing me in different ways for quite some time. I never told Momma because I thought she wouldn't be able to handle it in her weakened state. I knew she was aware something was happening, but she didn't know what. She asked me numerous times why I was so sad and I contemplated telling her a number of times but kept it inside. Several times, I did tell Dad I didn't like to be alone with Auntie Neely, but he didn't ask any further questions nor did he protect me from her actions. It was almost as if he was experiencing the same thing with Auntie Neely as I was. Whenever he could send me instead of going himself, he did. I thought a father was supposed to ward off any attacks on his children, but my father seemed to use me as a human shield for himself. I didn't know what that was about for a long time. Later, it all became a bit clearer.

Chapter 9

Sister Richardson anxiously awaited Demetri. Neely had informed her that he and Vanessa would be returning to Sunday School today after a time of adjustment and grieving. She soon saw him walking toward her classroom.

"Good Morning, Demetri," she said as Demetri entered the classroom without responding.

Sister Richardson watched as Demetri's classmates embraced him causing tears to form in his eyes. She noticed the deep sadness behind the tears before they even started to fall. She also noticed Demetri's appearance had drastically changed. Looking closely at him, she couldn't put her finger on exactly what was different. Finally, it dawned on her. There was no frame above his eyes. His eyebrows were gone. It was obvious he was a little self-conscious about it because he kept placing his hands there as if he had a headache or was feeling faint. When he had to use his hands for something else like hugging a friend, he moved his head in an effort to keep the missing hair from being noticed.

"Demetri come here for a moment. Everyone else, get your materials so we can begin." Sister Richardson said before taking Demetri by the hand and going just outside of the classroom door.

"How have you been?" she asked him, kneeling down in front of him to address him at eye-level.

"I'm fine," Demetri whispered, not making eye contact.

"Are you sure? I'm not so sure about that."

"I'm sure."

"Okay. How are things going at home since your mother passed away?"

"Everything is going okay. I just miss my momma."

"I miss her, too. She was a good friend of mine."

Demetri shifted his eyes to various places in the hall and leaned his body against the wall. Sister Richardson noticed his discomfort but wanted to dispel her concerns about the little boy's living conditions. There had been many times she noticed something wasn't quite right with Demetri even before his mother's death. However, since the funeral, things seemed to get worse and Demetri seemed more withdrawn. He had bruises he couldn't or couldn't explain and sometimes he would eat the snack meant for the entire class. Sister Richardson felt an increased need to pray for Demetri. All of the children in the church were permanent fixtures on her prayer list anyway. However, she sensed Demetri needed more individual prayer support.

"You know Demetri, I know how much your mother loved you. I can't replace her, but if you want to talk to me about anything you just let me know."

"Really?"

"Yes, really."

"Anything?"

"Anything."

"You won't tell Auntie Neely or Daddy?"

"I won't tell anyone but God."

Demetri reached out to his Sunday school teacher and hugged her desperately. Maybe God had provided a much-needed "ram in the bush" for him.

* * *

Chapter 10

Dear Demetri's Diary,

I remember that day like it was a few days ago. I thought God and everyone else had forgotten about me. Things were difficult at home and I needed help. Help I couldn't get from my father, Vanessa, and certainly not Auntie Neely. Since Momma died, I was lost. Sister Richardson became the one person I believed I could count on. Like she said, she could never replace my mother but, for me, she was close enough.

Chapter 11

"Demetri, come on over here and help me with my sink. I think there's something stuck down there and I can't get to it."

"Um, I'm doing something for Daddy right now," Demetri responded after being caught off-guard by his Auntie Neely's phone call.

"I don't care what you're doing. Put Julius on the phone."

Demetri knew he was in trouble now because, without a doubt, Daddy would make him go to Auntie Neely's house. That was the last thing he wanted to do. He had to think fast before his lie was uncovered and he found himself in even more trouble.

"Daddy's not here. I'll tell him to call you when he gets back."

Auntie Neely didn't respond for what seemed like forever.

"Your father's car is sitting right in the driveway."

Demetri resigned himself to dealing with Auntie Neely on his own. Daddy would not be of any help and he really didn't want him to find out about the lie he told Auntie Neely in order to avoid helping her with her troubles. After all, he knew the story. His family had to live here so they had to do whatever they could to keep Auntie Neely from putting them out. He hung up the phone and went next door to see what awaited him.

"Get over here and stick your hand in this drain. I dropped something valuable down there and your hands are small enough to reach in and get it."

"What am I looking for so I know if I found it?"

"Don't worry. You'll know when you find it."

He rolled up the sleeves on his shirt and prepared to put his hand into the drain. He didn't particularly care for doing so but knew he didn't have a choice. Auntie Neely had little to no patience whatsoever when she wanted something done. Demetri put his hand in there and felt a lot of mushiness that was undoubtedly food she hadn't yet run through the garbage disposal. It had probably sat there for days awaiting its fate if the smell was any indication. This was gross! Why would Auntie Neely expect him to touch all of this nastiness for this unknown item? The boy ran his hand around the gunk until he realized she was reaching for the garbage disposal switch. He yanked his hand out just as she appeared to be switching it from off to on.

"Did you forget my hand was in there?"

"No, I didn't forget."

"You were getting ready to turn on the disposal while my fingers were in there."

"Why would I do that? You know I wouldn't do that to you, Demetri!"

Demetri knew no such thing. Auntie Neely was unpredictable. He never knew what she would do. What he did know was he had to get out of here before he really got hurt.

"I don't know what you lost down there, but there's nothing there but food. I've got to go home now."

Demetri quickly rinsed his hands and turned to leave the apartment.

"Boy, you better get back over here and find my wedding ring!"

"What wedding ring? You're not married."

"Your daddy didn't tell you? We got married a few days ago. I'm your new mother."

"You'll never be my mother! You're too mean!"

* * *

Chapter 12

Dear Demetri's Diary,

They say into every life some rain must fall. I thought I'd had my share of rain. But, this was a monsoon. If my life hadn't changed enough already, it definitely changed with this revelation. How could Auntie Neely and Daddy be married? She was my mother's sister. I thought this had to be another one of Auntie Neely's sick jokes. This could not be true.

I ran home to find my father leaving the house. In fact, I ran right into him in my haste to find the truth.

"Hey, slow down, boy. Where's the fire?"

"Auntie Neely said you and her got married. Why did she say that, Daddy?" I said with the little breath I had left in my lungs.

Vanessa appeared on the front porch with suds falling from her hands and sweat dripping from her brow. Surprisingly, she looked as distressed at the possibility of Auntie Neely taking Momma's place as I was.

Daddy appeared to calculate his answer carefully. This caused me to believe I wouldn't like what he had to say. He looked from me to Vanessa and back a few times as Auntie Neely came onto the shared porch as well. She had a smirk on her face that said she was satisfied with her efforts to upset us.

"Neely, I told you I would talk to them in my own time and in my own way. You said you would wait. Why did you tell Demetri?"

"It just slipped out, Julius. I thought I lost my wedding ring down the drain and I wanted Demetri to help me find it. It was really in my jewelry box all the time. They needed to know anyway. I don't know why you pamper them so much. That's one thing that's going to stop."

"Vanessa and Demetri, me and Neely did get married. You know I loved your mother. I still do. But she's gone and I need somebody. I hope you understand."

I understood all too well. Hell is not a one-story building. It's more like a skyscraper. There are more levels to it than I ever imagined. I was about to be plunged even deeper into the abyss because now Auntie Neely was not just my aunt but also my stepmother.

• • •

Chapter 13

Demetri and Vanessa sat silently in her room pondering what they'd just learned. Undoubtedly, the shock of it all hadn't subsided just yet and the two had more questions than answers. Over the noise of their thoughts, they heard Auntie Neely's diabolical laughter. They also heard their father fussing at her because of how insensitive she had been in telling Demetri about their marriage.

"I'm going to run away. I can't live with her," Demetri cried. "She tried to turn her garbage disposal on while my hands were down there."

"What? Are you sure?" Vanessa asked. "That doesn't sound like her."

"Nobody believes me," Demetri spoke quietly.

Vanessa sat down on the bed next to Demetri. She hugged him close to her like their mother used to do. She allowed her little brother to cry. She rocked him until he fell asleep. Vanessa went to the bathroom and got down on her knees to ask God what to do. She was starting to believe what Demetri was telling her, though she'd never seen any evidence of what he said was happening. He was so adamant that she thought she at least had to pay a little more attention to what he was saying. Though she didn't acknowledge it, she believed him when he said he was thinking about running away. She couldn't let that happen. This was more serious than she initially thought.

"Vanessa! Demetri!" Julius yelled as he reentered their home.

Both children appeared wondering what their father could possibly have to say now.

"Look now. I know y'all are upset about me marrying your aunt, but that's the way it is. Neely is right. I have to stop babying you. Both of you have to figure out how to deal with it, because she's my wife now."

"Is she staying next door?" Vanessa wondered aloud. Maybe if they all lived together, she could get some help with the cooking and cleaning.

"We haven't figured all that out yet."

Demetri stepped forward. "Dad, I have to say something."

"I'm listening."

"I cannot live with Auntie Neely," he cried. "She does bad things to me. I'm scared she's going to hurt me. I will run away if you make me live with her."

Julius slipped one of his hands in his pants pocket and the other rubbed his chin. He dropped his head and paced the floor obviously in deep thought. No one said a word as he pondered what Demetri so passionately expressed.

"I know, son. I just don't know what to do. I have to be with Neely so we have some place to live. I'm not a young man anymore so I can't keep working like this to support us."

"But, Dad..." Demetri started.

"That's it, boy! I'll see what I can do to get her to let up some, but you're going to have to deal with it just like me. You think I want to be married to Neely? Well, I don't. Y'all actually thought I was just fixing her sink and taking out her garbage all those years? Well, she made me do some terrible and humiliating things I don't even want to think about. I wasn't jumping up and down to get to do that. She was mean to me, too, and still is, to tell you the truth. I'm hoping she goes a little lighter on all of us because we're married. If she doesn't, you're going to have to man up, boy."

Demetri and Vanessa were shocked— Vanessa because her idea of Auntie Neely was shattered, Demetri because he just discovered Auntie Neely mistreated his father, too. Julius left the room and went to find Neely to smooth things over with her.

Chapter 14

Dear Demetri's Diary,

We did all move in together a week after we found out about the marriage. Since Auntie Neely had the bigger unit and it was in better shape, we moved to her half of the duplex. She rented out the part we lived in so she wouldn't be losing any money on the deal. I didn't want to move. It felt like I was losing Momma all over again. All my memories of her were there. I also felt a little safer living apart from Auntie Neely. Now I had to see her all day every day without a door and walls as a buffer. I thought I was going to have a nervous breakdown trying to watch my back constantly. I knew no one else was watching out for me. Vanessa tried to, but because she was doing all of the cooking, cleaning, and even waiting on Auntie Neely hand and foot, she didn't have the time or the energy. Daddy did get the reprieve he wanted from his work schedule and Auntie Neely's treatment. This was no way for a young boy to live.

Chapter 15

Demetri and Vanessa made their way to their respective Sunday school classes. It was a welcome relief for them both after the week they'd had. Vanessa made sure Demetri got to Sister Richardson's class before she went to her own.

Once everyone settled down, she gathered them around to talk about Joseph and the various trials he endured.

"Joseph's brothers were very upset with him because of the dreams God gave him. They also didn't like that their father favored him. When they had a chance, they sold him into slavery," Sister Richardson taught. "Does everyone know what that means?"

"Yes" the class replied.

Demetri thoughtfully pondered that slavery concept as the class went ahead. He overheard something about "Potiphar's wife lied on him," "Joseph thrown in prison," and references to other bad things Joseph went through though he was innocent. Demetri focused on him being sold into slavery by his own brothers. He could identify with that. He felt his own father had sold him and his sister into slavery to Auntie Neely. How could his father do that? A father is supposed to make sacrifices for his children, not the other way around. Even after finding out what was happening, his father still allowed it to continue so he could save himself the trouble. Demetri didn't know how Joseph felt about his brothers, but he wasn't sure he would ever be able to overlook his father's lack of concern for him.

●   ●   ●

Chapter 16

The sounds coming from the bedroom where Demetri's father and Auntie Neely slept sounded as though there was a problem brewing. It sounded like somebody was getting knocked around. There was bumping, knocking, grunts, and screams coming from there as well. Though they obviously weren't concerned for his safety, Demetri didn't want anything to happen to cause additional problems. He made a decision to grab the baseball bat he kept in the corner next to his bed and head down and across the hall. He prayed there wasn't a robber or something in the house. The closer he got to the room the louder the sounds became.

He turned the doorknob, pushed the door open slowly—, and saw something he never thought he'd see. It looked like they were wrestling with each other, only there were no clothes of any kind involved. Auntie Neely saw Demetri standing in the room with his eyes bulging from his head and his mouth hanging open and never stopped the activity. She wasn't the least bit ashamed. She never even broke eye contact while maintaining the smirk she usually had on her face when she was doing something she knew would hurt. When Dad finally noticed Demetri in the room, he moved to cover the two of them, but Auntie Neely didn't allow it.

"Let him see what we're doing, Julius. It's natural. Maybe he'll become a better lover than Evelyn trained you to be."

"Demetri, go back to bed. Everything is okay," Daddy directed, clearly ashamed by the situation and his new wife's comment.

"Demetri, stay right there. Actually, come closer. You need to know what to do. Aren't you curious about sex?" Auntie Neely asked.

"Demetri! Go to your room!" Daddy shouted.

Demetri didn't understand exactly what was going on. He'd heard of sex but didn't know anything about it except what he heard his friends say at school. He just knew he was uncomfortable with the nakedness in the room. Since it was obvious he wasn't needed to protect the house, he decided to follow his father's directions and leave. When Demetri turned to go into the hallway, he saw Vanessa standing there with her

mouth hanging open. She grabbed her little brother to lead him
back to his bedroom.

Chapter 17

Dear Demetri's Diary,

This was just another example of how Auntie Neely emotionally traumatized us. I later learned that good parents are well aware that incidents like this can happen and do everything in their power to prevent them. Auntie Neely didn't care if she messed us up. She encouraged me to take lessons, for goodness sake! What kind of aunt would do that? What kind of person would care so little about an innocent kid to the point she would expose them to sex before they could handle it? I realized just how sick she was that day. I also realized how beaten down and defeated my father was. I could see that he was tired of fighting Auntie Neely for his dignity and obviously had conceded the battle.

Chapter 18

Demetri went to his secret place, his refuge. He felt embarrassed to face Auntie Neely and his father after what he'd witnessed the night before. He went out the back door of the duplex and down the driveway toward the street. When he reached the front of the house, he insured no one was looking and slipped into the area under the porch that was his hiding place. This was where he escaped after he found out his mother died, when his father married his aunt, and so many times after Auntie Neely did some mean and evil thing to him. This place had become his sanctuary. In a space where the floor was dirt and the ceiling was unpainted splintered wood, he found peace. A picture of his mother that he'd placed between some glued-together sticks to form a frame hung on the lattice separating the space from the front yard. He also kept a bible and a small flashlight to read with in the darkened spot. Today, Demetri couldn't wait to come here. He felt a need to pray to release all the frustrations of the recent past. He had some questions for God that could no longer wait. Momma and Sister Richardson taught him he could ask God questions while others told him he should never question God. He felt God knew what he was thinking anyway, so why shouldn't he voice his concerns?

Demetri pulled his knees to his chest, holding them firmly with his arms, and squeezed his eyes shut. He began to release the tears straining against his tightly closed eyelids. He felt like Joseph must have felt while sitting in that prison cell. Apparently, paying the price for guilt, though innocent, was something Demetri and Joseph had in common.

Chapter 19

Vanessa dropped Demetri off at his Sunday school class, as was their custom. She made sure his clothes were straight and his face was clean. Sister Richardson greeted the two of them as she normally did as well. The teacher noticed Demetri wasn't looking like himself and wondered why this was the case. He looked exhausted, as if he'd had to run a marathon to get to the church this morning.

"Demetri, are you okay?" she asked her prize student.

He replied with a short, "Yes."

"Okay. Are you sure? You look like you didn't get enough sleep or something."

Demetri lifted his head slowly and looked deeply into Sister Richardson's eyes. He studied her face for a few seconds. Finally, he responded.

"Don't worry Sister Richardson. God is going to deliver me one day just like he delivered Joseph. Just keep praying for me."

Demetri's declaration stunned Sister Richardson because he never referred to any type of struggle before. He desperately tried to hide whatever was going on though she knew otherwise.

Sister Richardson gasped as she realized things must have been getting much worse for him to speak so openly. The woman pulled herself together and went into the room. Just in the five minutes since her encounter with Demetri, he'd fallen fast asleep with his head on his desk.

Sister Richardson left her class and went to the room where Vanessa's class was in session. She motioned for her teacher to come to the door and asked if it was okay for her to speak to Demetri's sister for a moment.

"Did something happen to Demetri?" Vanessa inquired when she came into the hall.

"Vanessa, I was going to ask you the same thing. Is everything okay at home?"

Vanessa lowered her head before looking the woman in the eye and saying, "Yes, everything's okay. We're still adjusting to Momma being gone, but it's okay." Sister Richardson knew Vanessa was lying but couldn't accuse her of that. Both children obviously knew to keep what went on inside their house, inside their house.

"Why are you asking? Did Demetri do something bad?"

"No, he just doesn't seem quite like himself and I just wondered if there was something I should be concerned about."

Vanessa looked like she wanted to speak but thought better of it.

"What is it Vanessa? I can see you have something else to add."

"Ummm, no ma'am, I don't."

"Okay, well if you can think of anything let me know. Okay?"

"Okay."

Sister Richardson slowly began her trek back to her classroom. Suddenly, she heard Neely's voice and knew she needed to speed things up a bit. When she turned into her classroom, she saw Neely grab a sleeping Demetri up from the table by his ear. The surprised look on his face declared he was so deeply asleep he didn't even hear the woman's loud voice.

"I'll teach you to sleep on the Lord." Neely yanked him out of his seat, unzipped his pants, and pulled them down in front of the whole class, revealing his nakedness all while Demetri begged her to stop. She pulled him by the ear into the hall and judging by the direction the voices were coming from, into the girl's bathroom.

Stunned, Sister Richardson yelled out that she needed help and a few other teachers came to see what was going on. She pulled the teachers aside to explain the situation. One of the teachers stayed with Sister Richardson's class to redirect their attention, one went to get a deacon, and one went with Sister Richardson to be a witness to whatever atrocity was happening to the screaming boy in the bathroom.

"Sleep with the fishes, little boy. You know what to do. I'm not going to have you embarrassing me up in this church."

"Please Auntie Neely. Don't make me do that. I promise I won't fall asleep again. I promise."

"You should've thought about that before you laid your head down and went to sleep. Now let's do this so I don't have to miss my Sunday school class. Put your head in there."

As Sister Richardson and her fellow teacher turned the corner, they realized Demetri and Neely were in a stall. They walked in to see her push Demetri's head into the toilet. Sister Richardson had seen enough and snatched Demetri from Neely's grasp.

"Don't you go getting involved in this, Sister Richardson. This ain't your business."

Ironically, the deacon responding to the call for help was Demetri and Vanessa's father, Julius. Once he assessed the situation and realized everyone else knew what transpired, he dropped his head and began to sob. He cried like a man who had lost everything else and now his dignity.

"Neely, you are way too much pressure. What are you doing to Demetri this time? You making him sleep with the fishes again?"

"How did you know? That's exactly what she instructed your son to do!" Sister Richardson realized this wasn't the first time this had occurred and that Demetri's father was aware of it happening.

"Julius, you're a weakling. You're crying harder than Demetri. You think these people are going to feel sorry for you? They won't. They're thinking the same thing about you that I am. That you're a pitiful excuse for a man and I don't know why I married you." Neely exited the bathroom and wove her way through the crowd that had gathered outside of the basement bathroom.

No one said a word. All seemed to realize the magnitude of what they'd witnessed. The pastor, who had silently witnessed the scene, began to pray. The crowd began to follow suit as they sought God in that moment. After the prayer, Julius grabbed Demetri by the hand and led him out of the small bathroom.

"Julius, you and Demetri come to my office for a moment, please. If you can round up Neely, she needs to come, too. Sister Richardson I might need you as well."

Demetri seemed extremely uncomfortable about the current state of affairs and began to look around as his father led him toward the stairs to the upper level where the pastor's office was located. Sensing he may have been looking for her, Sister Richardson caught up with the pair and grabbed Demetri's other hand. Immediately, the young man's countenance changed and he relaxed a little.

Once those summoned were in the office, the pastor began to speak. It was clear he carefully planned his words.

"Brother, we won't allow Demetri to go home with you. We can't take that chance." The pastor stated calmly from behind his desk.

"There's no reason to think he won't be safe there," Julius responded.

"It looks like Neely is abusive and that's not a safe environment for Demetri or Vanessa to be in. If this was allowed to go on, someone might get seriously hurt."

"I'll be there to protect Demetri. He's my son and that's part of my job." Julius seemed a little offended that people would see him as unable to keep his son safe.

"Apparently you're not capable of that since you haven't protected him from 'sleeping with the fishes' on previous occasions."

"What makes you think I knew about that?" Julius questioned.

"You referred to it earlier in the bathroom. You asked Neely if that's what she was doing."

Neely was silent as the discussion took place. She didn't seem the least bit bothered by what others said about her.

"Look, I don't think I've done anything wrong. These kids are spoiled and pampered. They needed someone to help toughen them up," Neely commented.

"You think pushing Demetri's head in a toilet is appropriate?" the pastor said. "That's abusive. It's even more alarming that you don't recognize it's wrong. Julius, let me ask you something in light of this discussion."

"Okay, go ahead and ask your question."

"What are you prepared to do with your marriage considering all that has happened?"

"Julius, let me tell you something else," Neely answered as though someone asked her a question. "I don't want these kids. I never did. I don't even like them even though they're my niece and nephew as well as my stepchildren. If we stay together as a family, that won't change. Since I'm on a roll, I'm not sure what I feel about you either. If that'll make your decision easier, there it is."

• • •

Chapter 20

Dear Demetri's Diary,

Vanessa and I couldn't go home with Daddy and Auntie Neely. It was never clear what Daddy really wanted. He didn't act like he was all that upset about us not living with them, but he didn't push very hard for us to return home either. The church reported the abuse to the authorities and they prosecuted Auntie Neely for what she'd been doing to me. For some reason, Daddy didn't face charges, though he clearly knew about it and didn't prevent it. Since Sister Richardson was a foster parent, Vanessa and I ended up living with her until we were old enough and decided to leave her home.

Sister Richardson married a man while we were living with her. Though we weren't their biological children, they treated us better than we'd been treated since Momma died. He took me for baseball practice and haircuts while Sister Richardson taught Vanessa how to be a lady.

Daddy still didn't visit us much. I heard he was killing himself slowly with the bottle, but I didn't see him for long stretches of time. He stopped worshipping at our church after the incident so we didn't see him there either.

I'm still fighting a daily battle with bitterness. I even question God at times. He's the only One who can explain why this all happened.

I remember the story of Joseph played a prominent role in my life around that time. I know he suffered injustice because of his brothers and not because he'd done anything to earn it. I know he went through a lot. But in the end, he became the king's right hand man. When Joseph's family came looking for help because of the famine, his position afforded him the opportunity to help his family including his brothers. If I were Joseph, I don't know if I'd be willing to help my siblings. However, in Joseph's case, I would've gladly aided my father.

Chapter 21

My father and Auntie Neely were in a terrible car accident. Auntie Neely, who was driving, was able to walk away from the accident without injury. My father was badly injured. He ended up paralyzed from the neck down.

Auntie Neely decided she didn't want to live through the "for better or for worse" nor the "in sickness and in health" parts of their marriage vows. Days before Daddy's release from the hospital, she disappeared. No one knows where she went, but I'm sure she's somewhere hurting someone. There was no way she could be nice if she didn't get healed from whatever was hurting her first.

Vanessa and I received a phone call from the hospital asking us to attend a meeting regarding our father's discharge. When I arrived, I learned Vanessa decided against attending. She didn't want anything to do with the situation. I didn't blame her. I wished I had known I would have to face this situation without her.

I sat in the conference room and heard the information they felt I needed to know. Since Auntie Neely disappeared, someone else would have to be responsible for my father's care. I asked them what this had to do with me. Apparently, as Daddy's next of kin, they contacted us to ask if we would consent to him living with one of us. Vanessa was no longer under consideration because she couldn't even bring herself to come to the meeting. Since I was there, I was the only option available.

He could go to a nursing center, but my father apparently made it clear that was not what he wanted. How he could make such a demand given our history and his current predicament I didn't know. I asked if I could speak to my father alone before I came to my conclusion. They led me down the hallway to the room where my father lay. He turned his eyes toward me.

I stood next to his bed and looked upon the man who was my example of manhood. His bushy hair was more salt than pepper. The expression on his face said he was in pain, though I didn't think he could feel discomfort at this time. We silently communicated for a few moments before he spoke.

"Demetri, I want you to sit down."

I sat, not only because of his command, but also because the weight of the moment sapped my energy to the point I didn't think I could continue to stand.

"Where's Vanessa?"

"She didn't come. She's pregnant again and doesn't need the stress."

"So, she's still mad at me, huh?"

"I think so. We don't talk about it much."

"How do you feel about me?"

"I don't feel a thing."

"Okay. It's nice of you to care enough to spare my feelings by hiding the truth. I know you probably hate my guts."

"Again, I don't feel anything."

"How can you not feel the least bit angry at me after everything that happened?"

"I don't know what might happen when the numbness dissipates."

"Do you forgive me, son?"

"I did that a long time ago. Momma taught me to do that as soon as I recognize the need."

"Your momma sure was a good woman. I miss her."

"I do, too."

The two men sat in an awkward silence for what seemed like hours. Unspoken issues danced around the room serving as the catalyst for the tension.

"Since we're talking about things, can I ask you something?" Demetri spoke, breaking the silence.

"Sure."

"Why did you stand by and let Auntie Neely do the things she did to me? I just need to know and I've never asked."

"I thought you would have some questions about that. The truth is Neely was abusive to everybody, including me. There was a lot that happened that you don't know anything about and I'm not going to tell you. I couldn't protect you when I couldn't protect myself. I was sick in the head. I didn't know what I was doing."

"I used to always tell you when she did stuff, but you acted like you didn't believe me. You knew what was going on though, didn't you?"

"I knew but I didn't know how to handle it. Neely was always threatening to put us out and we just didn't have any place else to go. We all had to play by her rules or end up on the street. I thought it was better to deal with Neely than to risk that. You understand?"

"I can't say I do. Do you understand how what I endured affected me?"

"I can imagine. It wasn't that bad though, was it? It made a man out of you. Look at me, son. I can't do anything for myself and don't know if that will ever change. Believe me, I wish I had made some different decisions, but I don't get a do-over. Most people don't."

"I wish you'd made some different decisions, too."

"Well, I won't hold you too long. I know they told you Neely's gone and I'm going to need help once I leave this hospital."

"They did."

"Demetri, will you take care of me? I need you, son."

Demetri silently stared at his father for a few moments.

"I don't know. The hospital says I have a couple of days to make a decision and I'm taking each and every second of that." Demetri stood to leave the hospital room.

His father began to cry and scream, "What will happen to me if you don't help me? I can't take care of myself, Neely's gone and

Vanessa doesn't want anything to do with me. Lord, have mercy on me!"

Even with his father's tearful pleading, Demetri left the room without turning back. It wasn't a matter of forgiveness. He believed he'd already done that. He was no longer angry. This man was his father, for goodness sake. He felt it was his duty to care for him now that he really needed it. The bible said to honor one's parents. What does that really mean? Where does honor end? Did that mean he had to sacrifice the time his father's care would require? How far did God expect him to take this? He couldn't expect any help from Vanessa. She made it clear she wanted no part of this. She felt she made her sacrifice after their mother died. This would all be Demetri's responsibility until God called one of them home. Where was his father when he'd needed him? He loved him but wasn't sure he wanted to spend the next several years caring for a man who chose not to care for him. Was he willing to give up his life for his father? It would be a different situation if he just needed a place to stay. But he needed more than that. He needed around-the-clock care and had no resources.

Demetri needed to think and pray about this decision. As he started his car, he acknowledged how major this decision was. Yet, he was torn between doing what he should do for his father and doing what he wanted to do. As he continued to drive, his thoughts were still on his father's pleas as he walked out of his room. He was obviously afraid and Demetri didn't want that. During his childhood, Demetri had been afraid many times, but there wasn't a soul who cared about it, including his father. Demetri couldn't help himself, he loved and cared about the man. However, the man obviously hadn't loved or cared about his children. As these and other thoughts swirled around in his mind, Demetri became keenly aware of what his decision would be.

Chapter 22

Three years later

Vanessa placed a platter of chicken wings on the patio table beside the other food items. She stood back and admired the table-scape she created. The centerpieces, serving dishes, and the food itself were perfectly coordinated. Everything looked appetizing and smelled even better. She looked out into the sprawling yard where her children played and thought about the loving and safe life she and her husband provided for their family.

She walked through the sliding glass door and followed the voices into the recreation room in her home. She observed her family, Sister Richardson and her husband, along with Demetri and his fiancé enjoying the various games. This was indeed very different from how she and Demetri grew up.

"Hey, guys! Everything is ready. Let's go eat."

Everyone dropped what they were doing and stampeded toward the outdoor dining room.

"That's what happens when you're such a good cook," Sister Richardson commented as she embraced Vanessa.

"Thanks. I owe a lot of that to you."

Vanessa and Sister Richardson meandered hand-in-hand through the house toward the exit to the patio where the group was filling their plates. Feeling the family's excitement caused the two women to smile. Everyone simply enjoyed being with each other. This was family.

"Times like these make me think about Momma. I miss her so much," Vanessa whispered with her gaze on the clouds.

"I know. I miss her, too. I know she would be proud of how you and Demetri turned out. I know I am. How's your father?" Sister Richardson asked.

"Demetri told me Daddy's not doing well. They don't expect him to live much longer."

"I'm sorry, Vanessa. I didn't know. Have you been to see him?"

"No, and I don't plan to. I get more information than I care for from Demetri. He visits with him. I've seen him for the last time."

"I think you need to reconsider. He is still your father, you know. "

"Any man who allowed what he did does not deserve to be viewed as a father."

"What happened was unfortunate but, regardless, he will forever be your father. You should at least go and say goodbye."

"I have totally disconnected myself from him and all that happened. I'm finally at peace. There's no reason to reconsider. It's over."

"I think you'll regret not seeing him. That's pain you don't want to experience. You can trust me on that."

"The only thing I regret is that Demetri and I went through what we did."

"Have you forgiven him, Vanessa? That's important."

"I have. I know that's the Christian thing to do." Vanessa used air quotes to emphasize her words.

"I'm not so sure. You still seem angry."

"I can't stand him, to tell you the truth. That doesn't mean I haven't forgiven him though."

Demetri rushed toward Vanessa and Sister Richardson with his cell phone settled upon his ear and tears in his eyes.

"What's going on, Demetri? Is everything okay?" Vanessa inquired as she reached for her brother.

"Daddy just passed away." Demetri dropped his head and sobbed. Vanessa walked away as Sister Richardson comforted Demetri.

• • •

Chapter 23

Dear Demetri's Diary,

Though my father was responsible for the pain Vanessa and I experienced because of his weakness, I felt he deserved forgiveness, like everybody else. Vanessa felt differently. I was able to talk Vanessa into participating in planning our father's funeral. She didn't want to have anything to do with it until her husband encouraged her. He felt it would help her get closure. Getting her to attend the funeral was a different story. She only agreed to attend if she didn't have to see him. We obliged her so we could be together as a family.

My fondest childhood memories were when my mother and I had our special time. Snuggling up next to her made me feel safe and loved. Her absence magnified the unpleasantness happening to me. She always talked to me about God's purpose for my life. She told me there would be hard times but God would use them to bring me into my calling.

I realize, looking back, I had to go through the things I experienced. All I went through— Momma's death, the problems with Auntie Neely and my father—was not without purpose. God never wastes our pain. Now, I know there was no other way I could be equipped to fulfill God's call on my life. While there were terrible circumstances, I didn't lose my mind or my life.

Now, here I am walking in my destiny, my calling. The compassion I have for other young people who are experiencing the same things I endured drove me to get a degree in Social Work and start programs to help bring about healing for abused young people. Who better to help them than someone who understands what they've experienced? I can help them learn how to deal with the inevitable nightmares, the fears, the abandonment issues, and other results of abuse.

While I was in college, I met a woman, Rayna, who grew up in the foster care system. We became close friends because of our shared interest in working with abused youth. We started studying together and later worked together developing my programs. Our relationship grew, and a couple years after graduation, we got married. She is one of God's best gifts to me.

As I lay my head against my wife's pregnant belly, I cannot wait to be a father. I'll have to learn how to be a good father along the way since I didn't have a good example to follow. Though my experience with my dad was often negative, there is a positive outcome. I know what not to do when it comes to raising my own children.

My scars still show at times. That's when Rayna pulls me close, cuddles me and prays for me so intensely that it seems God Himself enters the room. She whispers words of love, encouragement and healing just like Momma used to do. When the pain of the memory subsides, we praise God together for the victory.

I believe there will come a time when I'll be whole again. That's my daily prayer. Until that time comes, I'll take each day as the gift it is. Hell may be a skyscraper with unimaginable levels and depths, but so is Heaven.

Questions for Reflection

What is your definition of forgiveness?

What is the biblical definition of forgiveness?

How does your definition compare with the biblical definition of forgiveness?

Would forgiving Julius require Demetri to take his father in and care for him?

Does Vanessa's choice not to have a relationship with her father indicate unforgiveness?

Does anyone ever deserve forgiveness?

Why do you think Neely demanded so much of Demetri and Julius' time?

What may have caused Neely to be so abusive?

What do you think motivated Neely to be so mean to her sister and her family?

What does Neely leaving Julius after the accident say about her?

Did Neely love Julius or was there another reason she married him?

What do you think about Julius' willingness to allow Neely to continue abusing Demetri?

Read Ephesians 6:1-4 & Exodus 20:12. Research the meaning of the word honor. What does it mean? Based on these scripture references, did Demetri dishonor his father after the accident?

Just like Joseph, Demetri suffered at the hands of his own family. Later, Joseph found himself in a position as an adult to be of help to those same relatives. How likely would you be to take advantage of a situation like that to exact vengeance on those that hurt you? What would you do? Would you care for a loved one who knew you were being abused and did nothing? Would you?

Dear Reader,

Thank you so much for reading *Hell is a Skyscraper: A Trio of Novelettes*. My desire is that you take away a message that will have a positive impact on your life. If I achieve that goal, I will have done my job. I know there are millions of other books you can spend your time reading. I am honored that you chose to read one of mine.

Writing a book without someone to read it is pointless. That's why you, the reader, are so important. Your recommendations, reviews, and social media "shares" and "likes" are like fuel to an author.

If you enjoyed this book, please consider writing a review on the online retailer website of your choice and tell others about my work. Also, visit me at my website, www.DarlissBatchelor.com. There you'll learn about my other books, read excerpts, see video and much more. You will also have the opportunity to sign up for updates which gives you access to exclusive content, early release information, discounts and freebies.

Until the next book,

Darliss Batchelor

P.S. You can also find me on the web:
Website: www.DarlissBatchelor.com
Facebook: www.Facebook.com/BooksByDarliss
Follow me:
Goodreads: www.Goodreads.com/DarlissBatchelor
Amazon Author Page: www.amazon.com/author/DarlissBatchelor